NO

OTHER

OPTION

By

Wm. C. Pond

ISBN: 978-0-6151-8183-7

This story is dedicated to all my Marine Brothers.

"Semper Fi"

A special thanks to Otto Buder for his encouragement and lifelong friendship. Without it this story may never have come to fruition.

Also thank you to Mark Hooper at Angel Editing for all the help in producing a very professional-looking piece of work.

LIFE
Life is nude to some who see
But life is what you make it to be
Life to some is a child to come soon
But Life to another is a thorn in the womb
Life to the old is day by day
But Life to the young is eternally gay
Life can be sorrow, pain and distress
But Life can be a mountain to climb to the crest
Life is what you make it to be
But Life is nude to some who see

Table of Contents

Foreword

This story isn't about psychology, sociology or anthropology. It's not about any of the 'ologies', but it does deal with the idea, specifically, that our actions and reactions are controlled by positive and negative response or 'self-control'. I remember reading the concept in Psychology 101, or was it Sociology 101? I can't remember, but it has played on my mind for years and was my inspiration to write this story.

The fact is, we control our actions and reactions as individuals or as a society by the positive and negative responses we feel when doing something. It is the reason criminals commit crimes or do-gooders do good. It is the reason we have penalties and punishments, awards and volunteer programs. But what guides our response if we lose control over ourselves? Not self-control, but the ability to control. Self-control is self-governed, based on the influencing elements of the situation, such as; greed, lust, addiction, honor or any number of predicating factors. Losing control of our situation can be self-inflicted, but is always unforeseen and frightening. Why? Because it is fear of the unknown; fear of no control of what lies beyond our next step or our next breath. Losing the ability to control our response to a situation usually catapults us to escape to our inner self or spiritual beliefs in a higher power. Even the atheist will cry out 'Oh God' in the midst of horrifying fear. We know how we respond in controllable situations, but what determines our actions when circumstances dictate that to regain our control, over fear of the unknown, there is no other option but to accept death over life?

PART I

TRAPPED

Chapter 1

Trapped

Date: Late December - Time: Unknown

It all began on a cold stormy night in Van Buren County, just South of Teapot Dome near Three Mile Lake, which is about twenty miles west of Kalamazoo, Michigan.

"Open your eyes, ladies, it's time to get up!"

Through wrenched jaws Bill cried out, "Damn arthritis," as he tried to shake out the cobwebs from between his ears. He could hear the alarm blaring in the background.

The voice in the back of his head persisted, "Time to drop your cock and grab your sock," but Bill didn't move.

Vague reminders of spending some quality time with a couple of old friends, Johnnie Walker and Jose Cuervo, bounced around in his head. *You know, the old woe with me, drown in self-petty bullshit.* The only thing that had gotten him was one hellish headache, and...this horrendous pain in his damned knee, his shoulder, his whole fucking body for that matter.

Again the voice ordered, "Turn off that alarm, Yates, and get up!"

"Yah, yah, I know," he murmured, but still didn't respond, waiting for it to stop on its own. But it didn't. Why wasn't that damned thing whining down? He tried to look at the clock, recoiling in torturous pain emanating from his shoulder, "Damn! What the fuck?"

"Open your eyes and look at the clock, Marine. What time is it?"

Yates tried to muster his thoughts amidst the cobwebs. He

felt cold, cold and wet. There was throbbing in his knee, sharp pain in his shoulder and stinging in his eyes. The pain was more and more intense. All conscious thought was trapped in the cobwebs. A nightmare. He wanted to wake up and end it all. It all felt so real. *Why am I so damned cold, cold and wet? What's in my eyes? Stinging! Why hasn't that damned alarm run down?* Bill tried to open his eyes gasping, "BURNING! A HOT LIQUID! Something's in my eyes..." He couldn't open them.

He felt himself trembling. His mouth so dry, he couldn't swallow. He tried to clear his head. Vertigo had spun his mind out of control. "Oh God, I have to shake this horrifying nightmare."

"Open your eyes, shithead. You've got to open your eyes!" He wanted desperately to rub out the burning in his eyes, but his hands wouldn't move.

"You can do it, asshole! Try harder!" He again turned to look at the cloc...Piercing lightning bolts shot through his left shoulder, sending him into a gasping cry.

"For God's sake wake up. Shake this AGONIZING NIGHTMARE!" Then he realized. He was awake. Lieutenant Colonel William R. Yates, United States Marine Corps, Retired, had no idea as to what he was waking up to. The cobwebs were still there, the pain was horrendous, the burning overwhelming, but where was he? What was happening?

Bill could feel himself shivering from a biting wind penetrating his body. His mouth was salty and dry, but he felt sopping wet. The piercing pain made him so sick bile was coming up in his throat. A blaring sound penetrated the steady drone on his eardrums. Anxiety took over. That sound always sent a message of fear. It wasn't the alarm. It was sirens! "Oh God, what the hell is happening?"

Yates could hear muffled noises through the steady hum in his ears. Sounds other than the sirens. Motors running, the clanging of metal on metal, a shrill whining wind and voices. Yes, voices. He tried to concentrate on what he was hearing, straining to block out the pain the way he had taught it for so many years, but the agony was too overwhelming, sending him into darkness.

Consciousness was regained to grueling pain. He couldn't have been out long; nothing had changed. The clanging metal, voices, cold wet chills, the whistling wind, but most of all... the pain. It was all still there, very real, and very frightening.

He felt water trailing on his face. Some dribbled to the corner of his mouth. Bill reached with his tongue for a drop or so to wash out the acid taste that had built up on his taste buds. It was running off his neck or below his chin, but definitely not from above his head. His mind flashing back to his boyhood in Catholic school. The story of the rich man in Hell willing to give up his entire fortune for just one drop of water. Instantly, panic took control. What his tongue had just tasted wasn't water. It was blood.

"Call out to them, Colonel. Holler to them, you've got to get their attention."

"YES," he cried. "Hey, help me! I'm hurt...and bleeding! I can't see or move! Come over here! HELLLLLP! HELLLLLP!" Yates couldn't hear his own cry for help. His voice was gone. All the strength of the body had been devoured by the pain.

He listened to the voices, hoping they were getting closer. Nothing. "Hey, damn it, I'm over here." Again, through the sounds of the whistling wind and the clanging of metal, Bill listened for any acknowledgment to his cries. He heard them coming closer. *Yes, thank God!* "I'm right here. I can't move!" he gasped, trying to holler over the hollowing wind and clanging metal. The voices were right over the top of him. A rush of relief exploded in the midst of his agony. The sound of an engine revving and screeching metal.

"Hello, hello! Hey, I'm over here. I can't see. I've got something in my eyes and I'm bleeding." Yates listened again for recognition. None came. "Hello...Help! I know you're there, just get me out of this place."

Bill's anxiety stabbed at his emotions as severe as the physical pain of his body. He was afraid. They couldn't hear him over the racing engine. But they were right there. Yates could still hear them talking, but it was all too garbled to make out through the steady drone in his ears. Again that sound of an engine revving, but this time it was accompanied by a sudden jolt. The movement consumed his body and again unconsciousness took over, the body's natural relief to suffering.

When Yates awoke it was to voices. "You shouldn't have done that. We needed to get them out first."

Another voice: "There was no time. We had to turn it over to get it secured. Besides, we'll need help for that." Bill's mind whirled. Thinking he couldn't bear it any longer.

This time they sounded closer. "Yeah, Bob. There's two of 'em in here. Better get those EMS guys down here. It looks pretty bad." Bill could hear another voice. It was too far away, too many other noises to make it out.

Then the closer one: "Hell, I don't know, we just got it on its wheels and saw bodies."

Again, the voice he couldn't understand and the reply from the closer one: "No, I don't think they're going to be moving. At least not on their own."

Then he heard the second voice holler. It was lower and more distinct. "Where in hell are the medics?"

"They're coming, Sergeant," replied the first voice.

Then there was a third voice: "Nice night, huh, Deputy? Any gas leaks? Movement inside?"

"No leaks that we can tell. Officer Murphy didn't see any movement either."

Bill could hear them working above him. *Thank God they found me*, he thought. Pain and fear was taking its toll. He wondered who the other person was? What the hell was going on? Why was he here and how did he get here? He'd obviously been in an accident or something. A sudden shift of his body shot unbearable agony through his knee and sent him gasping, "OH GOD, HELP ME..... I'M TRAPPED!" Then it was lights out... again.

Chapter 2

The Rescue

Date: December 21ˢᵗ - Time: 11:17 PM

The driving wind had picked up. A mixture of rain and sleet whipped the stoplight at the corner of Kalamazoo St. and Red Arrow Highway. Ice had been building up on the roads for a couple of hours now and there was no hope of it letting up, not real soon anyway. The forecasters were comparing this one to the storm of '75. That one closed down both I-94 and US-131. A hundred thousand homes were without power for over a week, not to mention the business loses, school closings, and accidents it caused.

Sergeant Bob Lemos got back to his squad car just in time to hear the dispatch request assistance to another accident. He'd just finished a domestic call on East Cedar in Paw Paw and tossed his parka on the seat next to him. It was his fifth assist request since the beginning of the shift and there was still over six hours to go. Lemos started the squad car, confirmed the assist, and flipped on the siren and lights as he turned south on M-40 heading for Paw Paw Road.

Tom Murphy was the first officer on the scene. A deputy that thought his first responsibility was to impress everyone with how macho he was. Bob felt this guy should have never made it into the force, but being the nephew of Senator 'J.' Monroe Murphy probably had something to do with it. In any case, he was a fellow officer and deserved the respect that comes with a uniform.

According to the dispatch, this was no little fender bender.

Fire rescue, ambulance and the wrecker service had all been summoned to the scene. They were there when Lemos arrived.

Bob exited the patrol car, spotting Murphy at the scene. A long cable had been affixed to a vehicle that was resting on a large oak some thirty feet below the embankment keeping it from plunging another eighty feet or so to the bottom the gorge. Lemos was now the ranking deputy on the scene. He made a quick assessment of the situation and took over.

The wind, whipping in sheets of sleet, made it next to impossible to see, let alone heard. Bob started to make his way down to the crash scene. "How many, Tom?" he hollered.

Murphy looked up at Lemos coming toward him. "Yeah, Bob, two that I can see. Better get those EMS guys down here, it's pretty bad."

"See any movement, Tom?"

"Hell, I don't know, Sergeant, we just got it sitting back on its wheels and saw bodies."

"Well, damn it, Tom, look! Is anyone moving, crying, gasping for air, spurting blood?"

"No, I don't think they're going to be moving. At least not on their own."

"Where the hell are the medics?"

Tom looked up with a squint, trying to protect his face from the sting of the sleet. He saw someone moving at a fast pace toward Lemos. "They're coming now, Sergeant!"

With his head tucked down to protect his face from the weather and speak without gasping, one of the medics shouted as he reached Lemos; "Nice night, huh, Deputy. Any gas leaks? Movement inside?"

"No! No leaks that we can tell. Officer Murphy didn't see any movement either."

The medics and Lemos went the rest of the way down the icy slope together. The footing was treacherous. The driving sleet held visibility to a couple of yards, and trying to talk created more gasping than words. By the time they reached the big oak they realize how bad the accident actually was.

Heavy wet snow was piling up by the minute. Lemos was concerned that the wrecker had only one cable attached to the car. One cable on a vehicle made today would be no problem; they are smaller and lighter. But this car was built back when they actually used metal, a 1950 or '51 Plymouth Station Wagon. Back in his teens he and his best friend would crawl in under the hood and have room enough to work on the engine. Those old boats could lumber down the road forever, just don't get it stuck. At well over 3000 pounds, it would take the varsity football team to get it out.

One of the medics called out, "Can we get this door pulled back? I can't get to this one. I need more light too. Get some more light down here."

Lemos turned and hollered to Murphy. "Tom! On the wrecker, get that spotlight. It's hooked up to the auxiliary battery." Bob muttered to himself as he turned his attention back to the paramedic. "Why do all the bad ones have to happen on my shift?"

The medic replied in a disgruntled tone. "Probably the same damned reasons it's always shitty weather on mine. Hurry up with that light, I can't see diddly squat with this flashlight."

Bob, responding to the command, glanced up through squinting eyes to see Murphy approaching from above with the spotlight in hand.

The sleet felt more like tiny snow pellets than freezing rain, and the wind wasn't letting up. Bob hollered over the wind. "Hand me that spot, Tom. The corpsman can't see with your flashlight."

The medic snatched the light from Murphy's hand before Lemos could hand it to him and snapped, "I'm not a corpsman. I spent my time in Hell with the 7th Marines in '91 when we went to the desert. But my personal lifestyle didn't fit their regimented beliefs and that, Sarge, was the end to my career in the military. So I said that old expression, you know the one, 'Eat The Apple And Fuck The Corps'. I didn't need them assho..."

"Hey!" Lemos interrupted, "if you don't get those people out of that car PDQ, you're going to think you were in Hell again with a 5-10 & 20! You know the old expression. That's five inches of this size ten boot up you ass, and it'll take you twenty minutes to get it out. Oh, and it's Sergeant - Sarge!"

The paramedic shook his head snickering and continued looking into the vehicle. Lemos wasn't in any mood to listen to some disgruntled corpsman make derogatory remarks about 'His Corps'. Besides, this was his fifth accident assist of the night, and by far the worst, and the night wasn't over yet.

Lemos felt uneasy for some reason, like something wasn't right. And if that wasn't enough, he had just caught a glimpse of Dave Marshall making his way down the embankment, hanging on to the cable for dear life, and still no victims out of the vehicle. He watched the sheriff gingerly making his way down the embankment. *What the hell is Dave doing here in this Godforsaken weather? What the hell am I doing here for matter?* he questioned. *I'm getting a good pension from the Marines. I got over ten years in my 401K, some in savings and a few CD's. I could've called it quits years ago.* Bob then said aloud to himself in the gusting wind. "I just love this beautiful weather I guess."

The snow was back to freezing rain again and felt like needles on Marshall's face. When the sheriff got close enough to hear over the wind, Lemos hollered out; "Damn, Dave. You're a real glutton for punishment coming out on a night like this."

Marshall smiled. His eyes squinting, head half bowed, still hanging on to the cable. In a gasping voice fighting a gust of wind, he replied, "You're probably right, Bob. Millie and I were on our way home from the Christmas Pageant when we heard the call over the radio. How many have we found?"

"Don't know yet, sir, the corpsman, (Oops!), I mean paramedic is just checking the vital signs on the man now. The woman must've died instantly. It appears her head went through the windshield. These old cars didn't have air bags or even seatbelts on some. They haven't been able to get to the back seat yet."

The sheriff replied, "It's damned hard to do anything in this storm."

"I'll let you know what we find if you want to get out of this weather for polar bears."

The sheriff looked up the slippery slop as he turned to climb out of the ravine. He shook his head as he thought of the climb back up and sighed, saying, "Do a good detailed report on this, Bob, and I'll look at it in the morning."

"It doesn't look real promising for any good news down here, sir."

"I'll catch you before you start your shift tomorrow afternoon, besides, we have something we need to discuss."

Bob didn't like the sound of that. He hoped it wasn't bad news about his son.

Suddenly, all the attention was drawn back to the crashed vehicle. "Wait, Dave," Bob blurted! "Fire Rescue has freed the male victim."

He'd been trapped on the steering column. Lemos and Marshall watched through tearing eyes for any signs of life. The medic looked up from his position next to the patient lying on the ground. "Well?" Lemos retorted.

The medic got to his feet and shook his head. "Too late, Deputy. No seatbelts to prevent him from hitting the steering column. Blunt force trauma would be my guess, but that's something the coroner will have to decide."

He turned back to the car and started climbing over the front set to the back. All the doors had been crushed in the accident. Bob and the sheriff could hear him call out to one of the firemen and his partner; "Get the front seats pulled up for a little more room."

As the paramedic wormed his way into the rear seat, they could hear him complaining. "More light, I need more light, I've found something." Murphy pulled the spotlight over closer to the passenger side back door. "There's a baby in here!"

Lemos, Marshall and the others moved in closer, trying to see through the honeycombed glass. Bob spit out in a gasping sound, as wind caught his throat; "Is it alive?"

The medic retorted in a frantic voice, "Hang on a second. It's under a bunch of bags, magazines, and stuff!" Everyone waited anxiously for the medic to answer.

"Here, take this flashlight, She's alive, I've got a pulse!"

A loud 'YES' rang out from the rescuers. The medic called

out to his co-worker; "Jackie, get some forceps and clamps from my box. Give me a neck restraint. Get the body board over here." After a seemingly long pause of silence, the medic cautioned, "Be real gentle." They quickly lifted the child over the front seat and onto the ground. The two medics tended to their patient for what seemed like a long time.

As they all waited for the medics to finish, Murphy shouted up the slop, "It's a girl," as if he himself had just delivered the baby. "It is a girl, right, Doc?" confirming it with the paramedic.

Not really paying attention, looking up for a split second from his position on the wet ground, he replied, "What? Hell, I don't know. Just be careful."

Murphy mumbled something, but no one was concerned with his rebuttals. All eyes were glued to the child. They had the stretcher basket waiting and lifted the small patient to the top of the embankment.

Dave Marshall, still with a death grip on the cable, obviously worried about his footing, asked everyone if they knew the victims. The only positive reply that made sense came from Murphy. "Well, sir, I've never seen them before, but from their looks and all that trash in this piece of shit they were driving, I'd bet they're a couple of those migrants that work for the Clayton Farms every year."

"It's not the season."

"I know, sir, but every year old man Clayton keeps a few good ones over the winter for a little help around the farm. That way he's sure they will stay on next year, and he doesn't have to pay someone to get 'em back across the border."

"Check it out, Tom, and give Bob your report."

Lemos followed with, "Okay, we all know what has to be done to get this area cleaned up. So let's get it done so we can get out of this Godforsaken weather."

Time: Unknown

The colonel regained consciousness; his body trembling in pain. Bill could hear them above talking about people involved. He couldn't understand who they were referring to. Who was with him and why hadn't he been rescued yet. He cried out again. "For Christ's sake, why don't you help me? Hey! Get me out of here, I'm trapped!"

"Come on! Think Marine! Think! The voice in his head demanded. *What'd yah got, shit for brains? Tap on something, scratch on something, get their attention! They can't leave you here."*

"Hey - I'm in here too!" He tried to will them to stop making all that noise so he could be heard. But the minutes became eternal, with no response. *They don't know I'm here too*, he thought. *They have to help.* He yelled again, "Come on! Help me!" Yates listened. Yes, voices again and very close now.

First Voice: "Get those doors tied down, Charlie, and make sure you don't damage that tree any more than it already is. I sure as hell don't want to lose this thing, then have to fish it out from the bottom of the ravine."

Second Voice: "I've got these chains secured. Is it in neutral?"

First Voice: "Yes, she's all set on this side too. We're good to go."

Bill, anxious with fear of being left along, hollered, "Wait! Wait! Damn It! I'm still in here. What are you doing?" Then the screeching metal sounds, an unbearable pain and unconsciousness - again. They were moving.

Chapter 3

Fears

Date: December 22nd - Time: 2:32 AM

The ambulance wailed steadily down Paw Paw Road on a one-lane path of ice in the blowing sleet. Henry Jessup watched his patient with anxious eyes. The bleeding had stopped. He had demobilized her leg and head, but what was going on internally was still a mystery.

His mind wandered back to another patient he had over twelve years before. The point squad was pinned down by sniper fire coming from a three-story building on the west side of Kuwait. The call for a corpsman rang out. It was Jessup's first real test under fire. The butterflies in his gut were churning, but he was determined. Henry knew in his mind he could save the wounded Marine if he could get to him in time. Hugging the side of the buildings and darting across the alley with Corporal Waddle, his escort cover, was no more than a faint memory now, but what followed was branded in his mind forever. He reached the third floor.

"Corpsman here! Corporal - Where's the injured?"

"In that room by the window. Keep down; we think there are more of them across the street."

Henry moved along the wall, staying away from the open window. He spotted an officer holding someone in his lap. It wasn't a Marine. It was the sniper. A thirteen or fourteen-year-old boy lying on his side gasping words that Henry couldn't understand. A round from an M-16 had ripped through the boy's stomach, his intestines lying on the floor beside him, rendering the enemy powerless. The sight of that boy invaded Jessup's mind time and time again. Faced with the reality that he couldn't help the boy, there was nothing he could do to save him. A belly wound like this was almost always fatal. Without a medevac, death was certain. Slow, but certain.

Henry looked at the first lieutenant trembling, cradling the boy's head in his lap. Beads of sweat peppered his forehead. A look of anguish in his eyes.

"Do something, Doc!"

"I wish I could help, sir, I wish I could help. We need a medevac chopper for any chance of saving him."

"Then he saw the lieutenant pull out his Glock."

Henry cried out, "NO! NO!" but he was being pulled away by Corporal Waddle.

"Let'm be - come on, let them be, Doc."

Then that flat piercing sound. The round from the lieutenant's Glock hitting its target. That sound still echoed in Jessup's head. Reverberated, knowing what the lieutenant had to do to keep the boy from suffering a slow, agonizing death. Henry knew the young officer's look for help from him was shattered. No more time could be wasted. It would put the Marines in fatal danger and compromise the mission. Crystallizing the decision that there was no other option. *So this is what the enemy really looks like*, he thought. A poor scared boy who had been forced into manhood, brainwashed with false ideals, and now begged for someone to help him.

That memory had been ringing in Jessup's head for over twelve years. The foreboding reality the lieutenant faced. The only way to end the agony the boy was suffering. The only option to complete the mission successfully.

"Henry! Hey, Jessup," Jackie hollered. "You all right? We're here, Paw Paw General. Get those doors open. We need to get this kid inside."

Henry snapped back to reality, but his fear of the Post-Traumatic Stress Disorder was also back. Each time it was as if it was happening at that very moment. He was shaking. Beads of sweat were running down over the prickling goose bumps on his cold neck.

"What! Oh yes, I'll get it." The trembling was getting worse each time the memory returned. But things were different now. He'd been making a difference every day since that day twelve years ago, right up till now.

Henry opened the rear doors of the ambulance and sprang out in one motion. The trauma team was waiting at the Emergency Room entrance until the very last moment to stay out of the storm.

As Jackie and Henry pulled the gurney from the back of the ambulance, the trauma nurse hollered over the whipping wind, "What've we got here?" as she came out to meet them halfway.

The Emergency Room doors swing wide and Jessup replied, "A small child. Vitals are stable, three lacerations on the right cheek and neck and a simple fracture of the right tibia, just above the ankle. No visible bleeding from the ears or nose."

"Okay, Henry, we'll take it from here. See you on the flipside, oh, and take it easy out there tonight, it's a bad one."

Henry watched the trauma team take the gurney through another set of doors and disappear into the examination room on the left. When they returned the gurney, a tense feeling come over him as if he was forgetting something.

Jackie closed the rear doors of the ambulance and moved it out of the Emergency Room entrance. She was truly a gracious lady that had seen the better half of her fifties. But it hadn't slowed her down any. She thrived on this work, loved every minute of it, and would do it until she dropped or they made her quit.

"Are you ready, Mr. Jessup?" she jested. "We ought to be getting back to the station."

"Just give me a minute to check on the baby, I'll be right back."

Jessup walked through a side door next to the Emergency Room entrance and down the hall through another set of doors and into the examination room to the left. Three nurses and a young resident intern were encircling the table in the center of the room. A bright light hung just over their heads. He could hear the soft murmuring of the trauma team at work, and the strained moaning of the child. He moved in a little closer, catching a glimpse of the baby between the bodies.

"How is she? Is she going to be all right?"

Not looking up the intern replied, "She'll be out of here in no time, a few stitches and she'll be as good as new."

Jessup smiled, but anxiety still swelled in his mind from his memories of the past. As he turned to head out the swinging doors, he questioned, "I still feel like I've forgotten something."

Time: Unknown

"Wake up, Colonel, you're going to be late for morning muster." Bill awoke to the nagging voice in his head and was instantly reminded that it wasn't work that was waiting for him, trying to block out the pain without success. His leg throbbed with every heartbeat. His shoulder had stiffened, agonizing with every breath. His eyes still stung, but watering or bleeding, he didn't know which. In any case the pain was secondary now to the terrifying fear of being left. Left to find his own way out. His torment overwhelmed by a consuming fear. "Oh God please don't leave me here," he cried. But no one heard his plea. He could hear that engine revving up, then several sudden jolts, compounding his agony to the point of nausea again. *There's that clanging metal-to-metal noise,* he thought, wondered what they were doing. There were other noises too, undistinguishable noises. Then the feeling of being lifted shot unbearable pain through Bill's trembling body. Darkness immediately followed.

He awoke gasping, choking and gagging from the taste of vomit in his throat. There were no sounds now, no engines running, no metal clanging, not even a whisper of wind. Just silence, dead silence, and darkness. Bill listened for what seemed like hours, trying to distinguish any audible sounds. He knew now he had been left. He was alone - trapped.

The choices are simple, he thought. It would be easiest just to give up and die. Freeing himself was probably impossible and would waste needed energy.

"Nothing is impossible. It just takes a little longer. You have two chances, Marine... slim and none, which is better than quitting."

Okay, expend some energy to gain mobility. Freeing himself would burn up energy, but it wasn't impossible or out of the question. So, it was settled, he needed to conserve energy, but without giving up and pray he would be found.

It would only be a matter of time before his battered body would perish to the elements. Growing weaker with every moment that passed, whatever was possible had to done, and done now, before logic faded entirely. Bill talked to himself openly. It felt like he wasn't alone.

Trying to assess his physical limitations, he pulled up on his left arm to see if he could free it. In a sickening grunt, he cried out "Oh shit!" *My shoulder, it must be broken*, he thought. Within the range of his restricted mobility, he could feel his left hand dangling at his side. There was no movement in his arm, but there was in his wrist and fingers. Bill could move his hand from side to side and downward, "Yes, down slightly." He concentrated on feeling with his mind. Blocking out the pain as he had preached to his men so many years ago. Reaching down as far as possible, knowing all too well where he agonized the most. His hand couldn't feel his leg below the knee, only metal. The forced movement was taking its toll and light-headedness seeped in. Whirling colors danced in his mind's eye in various shades of purple, green, red, and then the sick feeling again, just before blacking out.

"Open your eyes, Yates. Don't be such a pussy! Isn't that what you told your troops? Pain is nothing more than weakness leaving the body. No pain, no gain! Isn't that what you used to say?"

The voice in Yates' head was interrupted by a sound. He listened to hear it again. It penetrated his muffled ears, but he couldn't make it out. It was at his feet. Concentrating on the location, hoping to hear it again. Yes! There it was again. Only it was two sounds, distinctly different. Digging, yes, digging at his feet. He was anxious with the anticipation that someone was here. Again he heard them. "Yes, I'm here! Oh thank God you found me. I knew you would."

He felt a warmth close to his right foot and he laughed as a rush of adrenalin peaked with the thought of being rescued. Someone grabbed his shoe. Just as sudden as the rush he was feeling, pain took a hold of his foot. He shouted (more in surprise than pain), "Hey! That hurts damn it! Oh, sorry, ...just...just get me out of here." Again, the sounds and more pain. "What the hell are you doing?" He tried in desperation to make out the other sound. The digging again and yes, there it was. It sounded like snarling - like a dog. A Dog? Oh shit! *It's coming closer, closer to my ears!* There was more digging now, scratching, snarling and growling, yes, growling. The adrenalin rush was even greater than before. Only now it was from fear.

Date: December 22nd - Time: 4:15 AM

Sergeant Lemos pulled into Nell's Truck Stop on M-40, radioed dispatch that he was 10-99, turned off the engine, unbuckled the seatbelt, laid his head back on the seat and sighed. It had been a long night and it still wasn't over.

The weather hadn't improved much, but at least the County trucks were getting some salt and sand on the roads. The number of assist calls had lessened. Not as many cars were out at this hour and the smart ones were staying off the roads. Bob slowly picked his head up off the back of the seat and surmised softly to himself, Only a little over two more hours. He could handle that. In any case (right at that moment anyway), all that was in order was hot coffee and a bagel. Lemos grabbed his parka from the passenger seat and fought putting it on before getting out.

The wind was whipping with so much energy that Bob had to force his way out the squad car door. It was snowing, a dryer snow than earlier. It was sticking to the ground. At least that cold biting sleet had stopped, he thought.

Lemos looked in the window as he always did to see who and how many were there. It looked pretty quiet inside. When the door swung open, it almost blew out of his hand. Nell looked up to see who was coming in. Bob stomped off his feet, walked over and sat down at the counter.

"Hi, hon, you're late!" She frowned, then smiled. "The usual?"

Lemos nodded. "Yeah, but make the coffee black. The stronger the better."

"One bagel and strong coffee coming up."

He looked around at the patrons of the truck stop. A large bearded man was sitting at the other end of the counter, a young couple were in the corner booth next to the restrooms, and one obviously inebriated gentleman was seated at a table by the side entrance. Bob's first thought was the storm must have everyone hibernating, then he remembered it was two hours later than usual. He always tried to be there around the time the bars closed. It helped to discourage any would-be troublemakers that didn't want to call it a night.

Bob's thoughts wandered back to what the sheriff had said: "I'll catch you before you start your shift tomorrow afternoon, besides, I have a couple things we need to discuss."

Bob feared that something had gone wrong with his son's application into the FBI. Rick had worked hard on his studies in law enforcement at WMU. He was good in school and good in sports too. It had been his desire every since he was ten. Sheriff Marshall had put in a good word for Rick. Dave knew some insiders in the Bureau. Before being elected Sheriff of Van Buren Country he retiring from the Michigan State Police a sergeant at the Paw Paw Post. He also added: "But you got to realize, Bob, their requirements and screening is the toughest, and they only pick the best. We'll just have to wait and see." Lemos murmured, "I guess we will."

He didn't see Nell deliver the coffee and bagel. "You seem to be in deep thought, Deputy Lemos," Nell remarked as she plopped her elbows on the counter where Bob was sitting. "Anyone I know?" she asked with a smile. "What's her name?"

"Oh, thanks, Nell. No, I was just thinking about…a couple of things and an accident out on 41st Street. Just South of Three Mile Lake."

"Yes, I heard it come over the scanner, ah... around midnight, wasn't it? A double fatality, and a baby was involved. Have you been able to ID the people killed?"

Lemos took a sip of coffee and replied, "A married couple, but we haven't given out any names yet, not until we notify the next of kin."

Nell moved in a little closer, looked up at the deputy, smiled and asked in a low voice; "Who were they, Bob? Locals? You can tell me, and something about a baby, what's that all about?"

Lemos broke off a piece of bagel, dunked it in his coffee, then smiled. "Now you know I can't tell you that, but yes, there was a child involved and it appears she is going to all right, baring any internal injuries."

Nell stood up patting Bob's arm and went back to her work, commenting as she left, "Not even enough business tonight to pay the dishwasher."

Lemos finished the bagel and coffee without any further conversation. He stopped to pay the bill but was waved off.

At 4:45 a.m. the dispatch requested a check on an abandoned vehicle on M-40. The road crews had reported it. A couple of their trucks almost took it out. Bob answered the call. He wasn't expecting to find what he was looking at. It was a late-model black Cadillac. One of those sporty hardtop convertibles types that you never see around here. Not enough warm weather, and not enough money around here either.

It was hard for him to spot until he was right on it. It was black and there were no flashers on. It had been left unlocked with the key still in the ignition. Bob wondered who in the hell would leave this unlocked with the keys in it. He radioed in the tag number to check ownership on the registration and check for wants or warrants. It was clean. Bob confirmed the obstruction, agreeing it needed to be picked up.

The following two hours were the quietist of the night. A couple of people off the side of the road on Red Arrow

Highway, a disagreement in the parking lot at The Sportsman's Tavern, and that abandoned Cadillac on M-40. It was time to head in.

Bob's thoughts kept going back to the accident. The man and woman killed were the child's parents according to the report he'd received. Murphy had gone out to Clayton Farms as the sheriff had ordered. Their names were Felippa and Marie Lopez. The Texas State Police were trying to reach a sister from Larado. Her name was Mrs. Corina Romalez, Mr. Lopez's only known relative.

He wondered why they had been out on a night like this. Where were they going or coming from? Did Murphy's decision to turn the wagon back over have any bearing on the injuries to the child or the death of Mr. Lopez? There was something that made it different. Maybe it was the seriousness of the accident, or the weather, and then it could have been finding the kid. He couldn't put his finger on it. What was it? There was something, something to harbor concern. It just wasn't right.

Pulling into the station, Bob concluded it was probably the combination of all of it. With the shift all but done, he commented to himself, "I wonder what it is I've forgotten?"

Chapter 4

The Intruder

Date: December 22nd - Time 7:15 AM

Andy and Duke were making their morning rounds of the impound yard. Every morning they would take a stroll, checking to make sure the yard was secure. It was the best part of the job. No one to bother them, no wife to nag about this or that. The peace and quiet was tranquilizing.

The storm had passed with a fury, leaving everything covered with at least a quarter inch of ice. The snow had drifted and left bare spots in some areas and heaps in others. The local news report said that over thirty thousand residents in the county were without power and the schools were closed. Andy thought to himself, *What a difference a day makes.*

There was a nip in the air, but the sky was clear. The sun coming up in the east glistened off everything. All the trees, the buildings, the telephone wires, even the vehicles reflected back like a kaleidoscope of dancing colors. Andy reached into the inside pocket of his coat and retrieved a pint of Hot Damn. He took a healthy hit saying, "It just don't get any better than this." Then he tucked the bottle back in the pocket.

Duke had run up ahead for thirty yards or so, jumping and playing, sniffing everything and marking his territory. He stopped at the old station wagon that was brought in early that morning. Andy woke up around three a.m. from the sound of the wrecker's back up horn. His trailer sat in the back some fifty yards from the front entrance, inside the fenced in area. After twenty-four years, his ear was tuned to the sound of a delivery.

He didn't mind though, it was all part of their job, their responsibility, and their authority. Besides, Duke would always raise a fuss when someone came in. No one could get into this yard without their approval. Six or seven years back, teenagers would scale the fence and take parts off the cars. That had all changed since Duke had been around. He wasn't the prettiest dog around and he wasn't a pure bred. Just an old Rotty/Great Dane mix, but at two feet from the ground to the middle of his back and over 160 pounds, Duke saw to it that no man or beast had ever been allowed in without their permission.

Coronal Yates was alerted to a sound. *Someone's coming*, he thought, listening intently to hear it again. There was silence for a long period before he heard it. His heart quickened. It was those digging, scratching, noises he'd heard earlier. But this time there was a voice in the background, "It don't get any better than this."

Bill tried to shout. "Hey, hello, I'm here, in the car. Is there anyone out there?" His voice was no more than a cracking whisper. He strained to hear the voice again, but it was gone. "Don't go," he pleaded. "Help me out of here. For Christ's sake, please help me." Bill waited for a response. "Am I ever going to get out of this fucking tomb? Am I, Lord?"

Andy filled Duke's food bin in the shed, then picked up a few of his dog's treasures: an old radiator hose, a child's toy, and a shoe that Duke had found the night before. He tossed them on the pile with the other treasures his old friend had brought in. Andy shook his head then went back out to the yard to where his dog was.

He smiled, commenting to himself, "It's amazing the things that mutt don't dig up." He looked down and patted him on the back. "Yeah, I know this is your favorite part of the job too." Andy reached into his inside pocket and took out the bottle of Hot Damn. He unscrewed the top and proceeded to take a healthy hit saying, "Just you and me, out here all alone, breathing in the fresh air." Andy took in a deep breath but expelled it immediately, coughing. "Damn, dog! Ain't so fresh right now. Smells like something crawled up your ass and died old boy."

Duke knew they weren't alone. Their space had an intruder. He also knew he would get to them. One way or another.

Chapter 5

Remembering

Date and Time: Unknown

"Get away from me, you fucking mutt!" Yates' fears mounted with the relentless pursuit of his adversary. Thoughts of the pain, the cold, of being left alone, and now the tumultuous snarling and scratching of the dog were taking Bill to the point of hysteria. Tears of despair ran down his cheeks and he found himself praying. Something he hadn't done in years. He thought he'd forgotten how, but he remembered. As the words came, the sounds of the digging and growling faded, almost to oblivion. A serenity came over him, and then sleep, much-needed sleep.

When he woke up the dog had gone, given up. There was no sound. It was still. He shivered from the cold. The pains in his body still throbbed with every breath. The slightest movement of the left shoulder sent sharp pains to his neck and back. The colonel's mind was clearer now with sleep. That mutt didn't get to him, but when would it be back was the question.

Yates tried to focus on feeling with his mind. To determine where he was, and maybe break free. There was no mobility in the left leg or left hand and the left side of his ass was sore. That meant he was probably stuck lying to the left side. In any case, there was no movement on that side. The bleeding must have stopped or he would have bled to death by now. He was reluctant to try and open his eyes in fear of the intense burning. He knew something had gotten in them to cause that much pain.

There was an odor in the air. Wrinkling up his nose and breathing in as deeply as the cramped quarters would allow, he remembered that smell from before. It was oily or mechanical. The pungent smell strung a little, making his eyes water. It also caused slight dizziness. The smell was much weaker now than before, what was it? Antifreeze, that was it. Yes, Antifreeze from the radiator. It must have broken during the accident and gotten in his eyes. Was he trapped in the engine housing? That would explain the intense heat, the stinging and also the ether effect. Bill's confidence was raised. He felt he had accomplished something.

His energy turned back to the task of freeing himself. There was no feeling in his right arm. None! It could be just from poor circulation, but whatever, no feeling meant no pain, and he was okay with that. Yates pulled to the right side with all the strength his body could muster to free his left arm, gritting his teeth with grueling pain.

"You've got to do it. Don't give up now, you can make it. Come on, you pansy, you're almost there."

Pulling frantically, Bill could feel his eyes clouding up with tears. Light-headedness drove whirling pictures through his mind. Shaking and nausea came along for the ride. He pleaded, "Please don't let me pass out again, please God," and continued pulling. Then - SNAP! Bill felt the agonizing jolt of his shoulder pop back into the socket, and pain was now a constant entity, but it was free.

Bill relaxed, trying to minimize the agony and catch his breath. He tried to remember what happened before he woke up from the crash. His memory was vague and distorted. The Mexican family in the old station wagon. His car sliding off the road. A child, yes, the baby in the back seat. The old wagon hitting the gravel on the side of the road. Tipping and rolling. They stopped to help him out of the ditch. "Oh God no, they're all dead. No, the baby's alive." It was coming back to him. He wasn't going anywhere. Just getting away, away from the pressures, the separation, his work, from life in general. He wanted to be alone, just him and his two old friends, Johnnie and Jose. He needed no one, wanted nothing but to be alone. No one knew where he was going or when he'd be back, or if he'd even come back. He told no one about his plans except the bartender. Well, not his plans, his troubles to the bartender at the Ox Tail. He left San Antonio driving north on I-35. Driving for hours, stopping only for gas and to take a leak. He wanted only to be alone. *Well I got my wish.*

The colonel's thinking was interrupted by the digging sound again, and his frustrations exploded; "Oh shit...Go away, bitch! Get me some help. I'm going to die here if I don't get help."

Chapter 6

The Accident Report

Date: December 22nd - Time: 6:20 AM

Henry arrived at the sheriff's office at 6:20 AM. It wasn't part of the normal routine, but in a small community a double fatality doesn't happen that often. Jessup spotted the desk sergeant leaning over the front counter that was shielded in glass with only a small window opening to take care of business. He walked over to the window and waited to be helped. A large man, well over six feet and probably 260 pounds, stood up. He had a receding hairline and a pleasant face that gleamed with a quiet smile. Henry guessed he had been quite handsome twenty years before, but too many pepperoni pizzas and pitchers of beer had added a spare tire around the midriff. His appearance personified that of a gentle giant.

"Yes, may I help you?"

"I'm Henry Jessup, the lead medic that responded to the accident on 41st Street last night. I'm here to see Deputy Lemos. He called and asked that I come over."

The officer raised his eyebrows and smiled. "Oh yes, I'm the dispatch that called you guys on that one. Have you heard how the kid was doing?"

Henry answered with a smile while looking at the dispatch's nametag. "She's going to be fine Officerrr Kin-nop-pul-us, is it?"

"Yes, that's it. We heard she was going to be all right."

"Her right leg was fractured just above the ankle, a couple

of lacerations, and possible whiplash. There weren't any internal problems, nothing life threatening. Kids are more like little rubber bands than we are and they bounce back much faster too."

"That's great. You always hate to hear about any fatality, but when it involves kids it touches you more. I'll tell Lemos you're here." He pointed at a row of chairs along the wall, across from the dispatch station. "You can have a seat over there." Henry thanked the officer and walked over to sit down.

Jessup hated this part of the work, the pen-pushing bullshit. All the useless lectures, term papers and essays did nothing to make anyone a better doctor. He would have gone to med school if the AMA had given out doctorates based on ability. But Henry's decision to settle for paramedics' certification wasn't all that bad. He still got to do the thing he loved, helping people in need, and he was damned good at it too.

Sunrise was breaking through the front entrance. Jessup looked at the large black-rimed clock on the wall behind the bolted-down chairs. It was 6:23 when he sat down. The walls were painted a semi-glossy two-tone gray with a darker shade on the bottom and a black accent strip in the middle that separated the two colors. The walls behind the glass were the same. The ceiling was an off-white or just needed a good cleaning. The three large ceiling fans down the center of the work area hung still. The dispatch switchboard and work counter looked orderly, but the two office workers' desks were cluttered with papers, books and overflowing file baskets. The waiting area where Henry was sitting had a couple of florescent fixtures. One was buzzing and flickering randomly. The floor was also gray, only much glossier. In fact, about the only thing that wasn't some shade of gray was the broad yellow strip that started at the glassed-in counter and traveled down the long corridor before turning right at the end. It was a dismal-looking place and raised goose bumps on the back of Jessup's neck.

Henry waited another five minutes before seeing Lemos' imposing figure walking up the corridor toward him. He had a rugged handsomeness that Henry hadn't seen the night before. He was almost as tall as Deputy Kinnopplus, but didn't support the spare tire, maybe forty or fifty pounds lighter. From the scowl on his face, the deputy wasn't in a good mood. *Now there's a happy camper*, Henry thought, standing up with a bright smile.

"Good morning, Deputy." Thinking, *He probably hasn't had his bowl movement yet this morning.*

"You're late, it's 6:35. I thought you were going to be here at six a.m. I'm suppose to have this report on Sheriff Marshall's desk by now and the shift change meeting started twenty minutes ago."

"Yeah, I know, but we have paperwork too. With the damned American Civil Liberty Union, and all the other so-called do-gooders out there, if you don't cover your ass, you'll find it in court."

Lemos shook his head in discussed agreement. "Tell me about it, you need to C.Y.A."

"No, Sarge, it's not good enough just to 'cover your ass'. I think it's more like C.Y.O.A.F. - Cover your own ass first."

"It's Sergeant, not Sarge! Everything's done except for your review and signature. I have it all on my desk."

With that he turned, following the yellow strip down the hall to the door at the end. The strip turned right, Lemos went through the door with Jessup following behind into a large open room with several desks covered with papers and full file baskets. There were several maps on the back wall, a large screen pulled down and a whiteboard with several names. Some had been crossed out. Oh yes, that familiar gray moutique decorated the walls. Henry noticed at least three no-smoking signs posted, but the air quality was proof positive it wasn't a rule that was being enforced with any diligence. Lemos pointed at a plastic chair beside the only somewhat orderly desk in the room, and the three file baskets were filled to the top.

Bob picked up a folder from the desk and handed it to Henry. There were three typed sheets inside and a standard form with several pages.

"Here, Mr. Paramedic, read this, see if you agree. Want a cup of coffee? We're out of creamer. Sugar?"

"Read all of this!" Henry scowled. "Hell, I didn't think you were going to write a book! I'll be here till noon. I'll take that coffee, black's okay, and Sergeant, my name is Jessup, Henry Jessup."

Lemos replied in a joking manner, "Quit your bitching and read the damned report, I'll be back in a minute and I knew your name. I called your station chief, and by the way, you left at 5:35 a.m. What'd you do, stop to take a crap?"

Henry smiled and began reading saying, "No, actually to took a shower. It is what most people do you know."

Lemos made his way back to the coffee urn, stopping first at the men's room to take his morning constitutional. He liked this guy; down to earth, confident, or maybe he was just cocky, but spoke off the cuff. Best of all, Jessup had been a corpsman, even if he did have some kind of beef with the top brass. Bob didn't make friends easy, partly due to the job, but mainly because most people didn't measure up to his standards. Lemos prided himself on being a good judge of people and this paramedic was a real straight shooter. He had all the right qualities to become a friend. Maybe even a close friend, someone to have a few beers with once in a while.

He returned to the desk, placing a steaming Styrofoam cup on the corner where Jessup was reading, and sat down.

"Aren't you just about finished with that?" Henry looked up. Bob leaned back on two legs of his chair with his hands folded behind his head. "So you spent some time in the Corps back in 91? I was in from 74 to 94 myself. Made both Nam and the desert. Got out an E-8. Would've made E-9 if I'd stayed in for another short tour, but the wife was ready to get out. You know women," shaking his head.

"No, not the Corps, I was in the Navy," Jessup replied.

"I know that, but I won't hold it against you. Hell, the Marine Corps is a department of the Navy. We call it the Men's Department."

Henry continued. "I was with Force Recon at Camp Del Mar, out of med-training in 1990, the first year. After that I was assigned to the 7th Marines for another two years. I was offered a commission to take cadet training at the Naval Academy."

Bob thought, *"Oh shit, a naval officer."*

"But I got out in '93 when the Navy informed me that my lifestyle was not fitting to that of becoming an officer. You see, Sergeant, I'm gay."

With that tidbit of information, Lemos almost fell backwards in his chair, and Bob's renowned ability to judge people was out the window. Regaining his balance with all four legs of his chair on the floor, he snapped (more out of embarrassment than anger), "Are you finished? The morning shift change is just about over and I should be there for some of it."

Jessup looked down at the report. "Yes, I'd like to get out of here too, but I do have one question about how you found the vehicle. It was on its wheels when Jackie and I arrived. I helped the other deputy, Murphy? pry open the driver's side door. You state here in the report that the vehicle was resting on its roof. Is this correct?"

"Oh, well, you hadn't arrived yet when we turned it over. The car was balancing on that oak. So, not to risk it falling another eighty feet to the bottom of the gorge, creating even a greater risk for the victims, we decided to turn it over and get a cable secured to it."

Henry retorted, "Who decided? You know as well as I, when injuries are involved, it's S.O.P. to do everything possible to prevent any further injuries. I do believe that's the responsibility of the Fire Rescue Team, not the decision of some County Mount…"

"Deputy Murphy was the first one on the scene, and did what he thought was best in that situation. That is his job you know. Besides, it didn't make any difference, now did it? In fact, it probably saved the girl's life."

The medic thought for a moment. "I guess there was no harm done. Mr. and Mrs. Lopez died on impact and the baby is going to be fine. Just the same, it could have made a difference in the number of injuries the child had."

Bob handed Henry a pen saying, "But it didn't. Just sign the damned thing so we can get the hell out of here."

The irony of it all was, if Murphy had waited and the

vehicle fell from its teeters tottering position on the oak, it could be said that was what killed the victims. So, he was damned if he did and damned if he didn't. Jessup signed the report.

"That ought to just about do it, right, Sergeant?"

"Yep, Mr. Jessup, that does it. Oh, by the way, when you crawled over the front seat and found the kid, you said she was under some bags. What was that all about?"

Henry frowned as if confused; "Yeah, the back of that wagon was full of bags. Bags, magazines, and books."

"Could you tell what was in the bags?"

"No, not really, I assumed clothes, something soft anyway. It's probably the reason the baby wasn't killed. Plus, there were all those magazines.... I don't know, I wasn't concerned with it at the time. Besides I don't speak Spanish, let alone read it."

Lemos could see that Jessup was anxious to leave. It was too late to make the morning meeting and the report had to get on the sheriff's desk. It was time to end this little get together. He thanked Jessup for coming down and told him if anything came up that needed to be covered, he'd be in touch. Henry got up from the plastic chair and reached out to shake Lemos' hand. When Bob grabbed his hand in a firm shake, Henry smiled, winked and kidded, "See you later, sweetie."

Lemos quickly snapped; "Yeah sure. I've got your sweetie...Hang'en."

Chapter 7

Realization

Date: Unknown - Time: After Daybreak

The pain of Bill's failing body was fighting his logical reasoning with horrifying thoughts. His emotions intensified with anxious despair. Fear of the darkness around him and never seeing again. Fear of the unknown, where he was, how he got there, how bad he was hurt, and why wasn't he rescued? Fear of the known; the pain, the bleeding, the cold and that dog. Worst of all was the fear of being left, with no way out, to a claustrophobic death. Yates screamed in horrifying torment, "Oh God, help me out of this mess!"

"Try opening your eyes again, you need to see," his pestering mentor scolded. *"Come on, open your eyes!"*

"It hurts damn it! It hurts!"

"You've got to open your eyes, shithead, get your bearings. Do you know where you are, exactly where you are, Marine? Is it daytime or nighttime? Can you find something to pry yourself free with? Can you? Can you?"

"NO! DAMN IT! NO! YOU KNOW I CAN'T!"

"Good, know that you realize that, try opening your eyes."

The colonel began to move his head very slightly at first; a couple of centimeters in a downward direction then back up and from side to side. After a moment of rest, he moved his head down again, only this time as far as it would go, but recoiled in sharp pain radiating in all direction from his shoulder. Tiny beads of cold sweat formed on his forehead, and Yates sighed in exhausted retreat.

"TRY AGAIN, NO SURRENDER, NO RETREAT!"

Again, crimping his neck and head down to the point, his jaws wrenched, Yates felt something touch his chin. It was cloth; the cloth of his coat was touching his face. Resting a second, but not retreating. He wondered if his eyes could reach the collar of his coat to wipe them off a little. Forcing his head down a little further to the left was agonizing, but Yates obeyed, trying relentlessly to move his head to the left. *Yes! I did it. Now to the right.*

"Okay, now open your eyes, come on, open them! What do you see? Anything? Anything at all?"

"No! Nothing, damn it, nothing. Blur, just blur."

The menacing voice in his head was relentless. Badgering him to continue for what seemed like hours. Trying to open his right eye was hopeless, nothing to solidify the evidence of sight. Just darkness. The pain was too overwhelming and Bill needed to rest, to stop, relax, to give up. Closing his eyes so tight, he could hear the pressure on his eardrums. With his eyes tightly squeezed, he thought for a second. Wait, Blurry gray shadows. *If I can see shadows, I'm not blind. Not totally blind.* He uttered a sigh of hope that he had some sight in his left eye. At least there was some measure of light. It was a ray of hope.

"Good, now open it again, take it slow and easy. Give it a rest, some time to adjust. A few minutes to focus." The excitement Yates was feeling tried his patience. It was taking too long.

"Patience is a virtue. All good things come to those who wait. So hold your damned horses, Colonel, and be patient."

A few minutes passed then Bill shouted, "Yes! Focusing, it's focusing. A blurring light." *Christ*, he thought, *don't let me start crying now. It's a light. A beam of light.* He forced his head down again through the stabbing pain to wipe the tears away and see more clearly.

Bill's eye was focused on a small hole projecting a beam of sunlight. It was like a small spotlight that illuminated shadows across a stage of mangled metal. He looked up and saw more metal and hoses and maybe wires. He looked down but could only see his coat. Shifting to the right, the bridge of his nose blocked most of his field of vision. Able to turn to the right a little he could see more hoses and wires come into view, and a hole or vent of some kind. He switched his direction to the left, laughing inside with relief and reveled in the fact that he could see. He wasn't blind. It was darker to the left where the light was coming from. As Bill's eye adjusted to the shaded area, it appeared wet, oily wet. Straining to get a better look at the ground, a piece of wood, a bowl or cup came into view, and something else partially buried.

Closing his eye, envisioning what he had seen focusing through the blur and the tears. Bill became complacent, knowing where his claustrophobic tomb was. Even the throbbing agony of his body seemed to subside. He was in the engine housing up under the dash, thrown through the firewall ending up pinned between the heat vent and motor or something. The memory of watching a Ripple's believe it or not show reflected in his mind, where a man had spent several days in a small box. He didn't find much comfort in that. The warmth of the sun was working its way through the twisted metal to his cold aching body. He wanted only to sleep.

Chapter 8

Discoveries

Date: December 22nd - Time: 4:25 PM

The Van Buren County Storage Yard is located on 64th Street North of Lawton. It is operated by Andrew Sharpe. It was just him now since his wife passed in '05. Well, him and his dog, Duke. They were both big, rugged, strenuous, and not real bright; although Duke may have the upper hand in that area.

Each morning at 7:30 Andy opened up for business, spending his time making rounds of the property, checking the fence line for holes, picking up trash, reading the paper and talking to customers in the office. Then every evening at 4:30, Andy let Duke out of the shed, where he waited for his master to fill his food bin and put fresh water in his pale. Then they made their last rounds together for the night. Duke was then left in charge of the yard.

The next morning at 7:30, Duke went back to the shed to be fed and sleep out the day. This had been the routine for over twenty years for Andy and six for Duke. Duke's daddy and granddaddy had been on the job the fourteen years before him. Yes, he had come from a long line of junkyard dogs, and he was proud of it.

On this particular day he'd been fussing for hours. Andy opened the door to the shed and Duke bolted for the yard, knocking Andy over.

"Damn it, dog! What the hell's wrong with you?" Andy shook his head, smiled, then went to his business of filling the food bin, getting him fresh water, and picking up a piece of cardboard that Duke had been chewing on. He finished his chores in the shed and went out to start the evening tour of the yard, but Duke wasn't there waiting for him. Andy scanned the property and spotted his partner digging and scratching the ground by the old Plymouth wagon that was brought in the night before.

"Duke! Duke, come on, it's time to go to work!" The dog didn't move. *Hmm, I wonder what's gotten into him?*

"Here, boy. Come on." Duke still didn't obey, but kept digging. Andy walked in the direction of his dog.

"Quit that playin' around and get over here. What'd you do, find a critter hidin' in there? Come on, Duke, you can get it later."

Andy saw his partner look up and start coming to him, but instead of running ahead as usual, he grabbed the bottom of Andy's coat and started pulling. "No! I don't have time to look right now. Now quit tugging Duke. Let go of my coat. There's no time to be playin' around." Duke let go of his master's coat and went back to his post by the vehicle.

Andy followed to fetch his dog. "Christ almighty, dog, you'd think you found some buried treasure or something." Reaching down, he grabbed his collar and yanking as hard as he could, but the dog didn't budge. "You better come with me right now or I'll put you ass in the shed for the night. Now go to work. With that, the dog ran ahead and Andy followed, checking the fence line, picking up a beer bottle and taking a couple of hits off his Hot Damn before padlocking the front gate.

"Okay, I'll pet yah, you big old mutt. Take care of things out here and I'll see you in the mornin'."

As Andy walked back to his trailer he saw his dog returning to the old wagon. He looked at the clear sky thinking about how bad the night before had been with the storm. The wind had died to a calm whisper and the temperature had reached forty-two degrees by the late afternoon. The weather report said it was going to be cold and clear tonight. Andy thought, as he took another sip of Hot Damn, *Don't look like rain, but that's not what my arthritis is telling me,* which was usually better than the forecasters.

Time: Before Sundown

Colonel Yates lay amidst the mangled mass of metal. Despair consuming his mind as he watched the tiny ray of sunlight move across a twisted stage. He watched it come and go, in various degrees, from radiant to subdued. Each time it changed, so did the warmth and comfort that it released. Bill's menace hadn't been back, and he hoped it had gone for good, The voice he heard talking to the dog had gone too. Nothing but silence. A wisp of wind was all that was left.

He was alone, forsaken, with no hope. All of the prayers he had said as a boy had left him years ago. The years of catechism classes and First Communion were long forgotten. Bill remembered his acceptance of the Holy Spirit; the warm peaceful feeling overflowing from his body. That purity of the soul hadn't been felt in years. He remembered the Bible story of Job. The trials and tribulations he endured. It was all an idiotic ideology. All that crap about the Lord would never leave you. Never allow more cross than you could bear. He had left God behind years ago. The years, the times, the successes and failures left no room for any of that nonsense. *So how could I expect God to answer my call?* he thought. *How could I ever expect Him not to leave me?*

"LORD! You were there for Job," Bill cried out. "Why not for me?"

"He is here for you."

"God never left Job!"

"No, but why didn't He leave Job?"

"I don't know, who cares?" Bill sighed.

"Because Job never lost his belief in God, and neither have you."

Bill watched the tiny beam glimmering through the small hole, moving across his field of vision. He knew what time it was by the faint light through the hole he'd been watching. The temperature was dropping. The shivering had returned. The cold reentering his body told him the tiny ray of sunshine would soon be snuffed out by the night. It was the second night he would have to endure. All that was left was a flicker of sunlight. The warmth it had brought seemed to bring with it some hope. A false hope, he thought, as the cold seeped deeper into his body. He could feel the warmth being plucked away. Pinched out like a candle to an eternity of darkness and cold, so damnably cold.

December 22nd - 5:55 PM

Andy hung his coat on the nail by the door and hit the power button on the remote while looking at the clock on the counter. It was time for the evening news to start. Channel 3 was the local station and 8 was out of Grand Rapids. A coffee and some brandies were also on order to take the chill off. He would spend the news hour switching channels back and forth during the commercials and when the sports coverage came on. It was the regular routine, but this night was special. There would be complete coverage of the storm and the accident on 41st Street. Andy fixed a coffee and brandy, took out a fresh tin of *Grizzly Mint* from the refrigerator and plopped down in his Lazy Boy. He could hear Duke barking out on the property. The coverage of the double fatality was the lead story, blaming the storm for the accident.

"Icy roads are being blamed for claiming the lives of two people and injuring a child in Van Buren County last night. Officials from the Van Buren County Sheriff's Office said it happened on 41st Street North of Paw Paw Road around midnight.

"The 1951 station wagon slide off the road, crashing through the metal guardrail, then plummeting thirty feet, where it came to rest against a large oak, keeping the vehicle from falling another eighty feet to the bottom of the ravine.

"The names of the victims are being withheld for notification to next of kin. We have been able to ascertain that the two people that died in the accident were migrant workers from Clayton Farms, a well-known fruit grower in the area. No one from Clayton Farms was available for comment.

"The child (a six or seven-month-old girl) was treated for injuries at the scene and taken to Paw Paw General where she has been reportedly placed in guarded condition.

"A spokesperson from the Fire Rescue team said that the vehicle was not equipped with seatbelts. Also, that hitting the large oak (which kept the car from crashing to the bottom of the ravine) is probably what saved the life of the child.

"Last night's ice storm caused over fifty thousand Kalamazoo and Van Buren County residents to be without elect..."

Andy got up from his Lazy Boy to make another coffee and brandy. His dog was still barking. He looked out the kitchen window. The yard's automatic light sensors had just come on. He watched Duke digging at that old wagon. *What the hell's come over him*, he thought. *He's been a fussing at that car ever since I let him out.* "Crazy old mutt," he smiled, turning to sit back down to do some channel surfing.

Time: 6:10 PM

Duke's pursuit was undaunted by the frozen clay ground. The intruder had to pay the price for invading his territory. Bill pulled his foot up as high as he could. The protection of his isolation chamber wouldn't last long. He needed an equalizer, something to even the odds. Yates tried to see something. Anything, anything at all that would give him some hope of keeping his adversary at bay. The gray shadows ran together, making it impossible to distinguish anything. It was dark now, but that wouldn't stop the enemy. He was relentless. Bill closed his eye, hoping it would ease the pain from straining to see. In a minute he would try again.

He opened his eye for a second round, there was a faint light coming from the small hole above him. Yates turned his head as far as possible, moving his eye from side to side to look at the surroundings. The light was also reflected off the ground underneath him.

"Wait! Focus your eye, Bill," the voice commanded. *"What's that?"*

He could see something wedged down there. He strained to focus, but without both eyes all depth perception was gone. There was something there he had seen before but forgotten about. It looked different, not metal or plastic.

"Can you reach it? Reach down!"

I can't, he thought. *The pain in my shoulder is too great.*

"You have to try. Stretch, just a little." Bill obeyed the command.

"A little further, you're almost there. Yes, there it is. It's round."

"Get a hold of it. Pull it out, come on, pull! Here it comes. A little more, just a little more."

"No use, it's stuck," he mumbled, releasing his grip. Yates' energy was gone.

The sounds of digging had stopped. Sleep before the cold set in. Rest, it would be here soon. And so would the enemy, digging closer. Hurry numbness. He tried to will the numbness to return to his body to fight the cold. Hurry sleep. The numbness did not, but sleep did.

Chapter 9

The XLR-V

Date: December 22nd - Time: 4:35 PM

K in handed the report to Bob when he walked past the front counter, "Have you thought any more about what your plans are, Bob?"

Bob looked up for a second before heading down the hall. "No, not yet. I'm talking with Sheriff Marshall before I head out tonight."

Lemos cleared off a spot on his desk, laid down the report and proceeded to the coffee urn. He came in early to talk with Sheriff Marshall. Dave had mentioned the night before he had something to discuss with him, and it had been on his mind all day. Bob returned, picked up the report, sat down and began to read. It was the activity summery of the previous day, which included his shift for the night before. It had been a busy twenty-four hours.

He picked up the phone and punched up the County garage. It rang several times before anyone answered.

"County garage, Frank Rocha speaking."

"Frank, Bob Lemos here. I was wondering if anyone claimed that abandoned black caddy yet?"

"Just a sec, Sarge, I'll check."

While Bob waited for Rocha to return, he wondered what the sheriff wanted to talk about. He hoped it wasn't bad news concerning Rick's application into the FBI. He heard the receiver being picked up.

"No, it's parked in B-12 for claiming. That is one nice set

of wheels. Do you want me to move it? I could bring..."

Lemos interrupted, "No, no, that won't be necessary. I was just curious as to what the property report said was in it."

Frank checked the property report and began reading it to Lemos. "The front seat had a necktie, a scarf, two Garth Brooks CD's, and an empty liquor bottle, that must have spilled on the seat from the smell it left. In the glove box there were two maps, a can opener, a small pocketknife, some pictures and the owners manual. In the rear of the car there was nothing of interest; two paper cups, a McDonald's wrapper and the top to the bottle in the front seat. The compartment in the armrest had $1.75 in quarters, a candy wrapper, and three more C&W CD's."

"What about the trunk, Frank?"

"Ah! In the truck, other than the usual jack, spare, etc. There are two suitcases, a bag of chips and get this, a box with six bottles of tequila and four bottles of the same brand hooch that is in the front seat. They must've been going to one helluva Christmas party. Oh yes, the key was still in the ignition."

"I know, I checked it out last night during the storm. You would think it'd be picked up by now. What would something like that cost Frank, forty, fifty thousand?"

Rocha chuckled. "No, that's a Cadillac XLR-V Hardtop Convertible. It comes fully loaded. I think you'd be closer to guess eighty or ninety thousand."

"Wow We! Too damned nice to be sitting on the side of the road with the keys in it."

"You sure as hell got that right, Sarge."

"Thanks for the help, Frank. Oh yes, it's Sergeant not Sarge."

"Oops! Sorry, I always forget. You're an Ex-Marine."

"No. A former Marine."

"See yah, Sergeant, it's almost 'Miller Time' for me, and Merry Christmas."

Sheriff Marshall walked into the deputy's bay heading straight for Lemos. "Bob, you got a minute? I'd like to talk with you."

Lemos smiled saying, "Sure, Chief, what can I do for yah?"

The sheriff took a quick glance around the room and said, "Come down to my office, we can talk more privately there."

Bob got up from his desk. He turned to follow the sheriff, who was already halfway to the door. *Damn, This must be important and he doesn't look real happy. This may not be the best time to ask for a consideration to under sheriff.*

The word was out that Under Sheriff Knapp was taking a position with Detroit Metro. Bob told Kinnopplus he had thoughts about retiring, but he would like to stay on with the department if he could. Sheriff Marshall stayed ahead of him all the way to his office door, then waited for Bob to catch up. Dave opened the door, closing it behind them.

"Sit down, Lemos. What the hell is this shit about you retiring? I don't like getting my information third shiter from the left. I want to hear it first and from the horse's mouth. Now, we need to talk about this some."

Bob smiled and sighed, "You must have been talking with Kinnopplus, and that is not what I told him. Well... not actually, anyway. I'll have twelve years with the department in twenty-three months. Hell, I was here before Cal was sheriff."

"So, what is it? You want an early out, off the beat?"

"Oh no, it's not that, I was just..."

"I would like you to reconsider, Bob. Something's come up that you should know, but I must have your word it will be kept strictly on the QT."

"Of course, Dave, I understand."

"Jub Knapp is resigning in three months to take a position with the Detroit Metro Squad. That going to leave an opening for a new under sheriff. I had planned to recommend you. Of course, it's not quite that easy. The County Board would have to approve it, along with a few other requirements, but you've got a great record here and I don't see any stumbling blocks."

The sheriff waited for some kind of a response, but when none came he stood up, walked around the desk and sat on the corner.

"You don't have to make any commitments right now, take some time to think it over, talk to Mary and Rick. You realize there would be a big jump in compensation, and the position carries a few other perks as well."

Lemos shook his head, saying, "Yes, I'll do that, Dave. I'm going over to Mary's tomorrow to celebrate the holiday with her and Rick. I'll talk to them then." He stood up and turned toward the door.

Marshall was confident that he had swayed Lemos into staying on. Bob was glad he didn't try to sway Dave into letting him stay on. Bob surmised that all was well in Smallville.

The sheriff stood up and returned to his chair. "Good. Well, if there's nothing else, I have some BBS to attend to."

Lemos gave the sheriff a long puzzled look. Dave smiled, "You know, the bureaucratic bullshit," looking at the papers in front of him.

"There is one thing, sir. Last night on my way to that accident on 41st Street I passed a vehicle off to the side of the road on M-40, about two miles North of C.R.358. I didn't think much of it then. But after we finished up at the accident, a request came across to check it out. The road crews almost hit it when they were working the area. When I got there, I found out why. It's black, one of those small sports models they just came out with. I had the plates ran and it checked out fine. The strange thing is, it was unlocked. I called the County garage to get it towed."

"So what's the problem?"

"Well, sir, I called the garage when I came in, and it still hasn't been claimed. It seemed awfully careless that anyone would leave a ninety-thousand-dollar vehicle seating alongside the road."

"A ninety-thousand-dollar automobile? What the hell?"

"There aren't any wants or warrants on the registered owner, and it isn't on the hot sheet, but get this, Dave, the keys were still in the ignition."

"That does sound peculiar. All right, I'll have Jub do some checking. With the storm as bad as it was, they could be out there yet. They probably went to one of the residences in the area, but it won't hurt to check it out."

Marshall followed the deputy to the office door. "Have a

happy holiday, and thanks for coming in early."

"No, thank you. It's no problem, Dave, I was coming in early anyway. My last night before the weekend and the nightshift for a month." Bob looked at his watch and started down the hall.

"I'd better get my ass moving, rotation meeting in five. Oh! - and have a Merry Christmas, Sheriff."

Chapter 10

The Shoe

Date: Unknown - Time: An eternity of night

"LET GO OF ME, you son of a bitch!" Bill's adversary wouldn't let go. The enemy was fighting Bill for what was rightfully his. But Yates was trespassing on the mutt's territory.

"Think Bill, try talking nice to him, in a subtle tone."

"Come on, be a good boy and go screw yourself." It didn't work. His opponent had a death lock on his foot.

"You've got to pull it up! Get it up, Colonel, before he tears your damn foot off."

KALUNK! The pressure instantly stopped, causing his leg to recoil. The tug of war had ended. The weakest link in the chain had broken. A surge of cold air hit Bill's foot. He'd lost the battle. That persistent bastard had his shoe, leaving his foot open to the attack. But suddenly the digging, and the low determined growl stopped. There was a faint sound of wheels rolling on gravel. An engine running, the unmistakable sound of a car door closing. He could tell it was still dark from the glow of the hole above him and the reflection on the ground underneath, but mostly from the cold that darkness brings. He rested from his fight with fears, knowing it would be back. Knowing the next time it would be flesh - his flesh. He lay motionless, breathing in deep slow breaths to relax his tenuous body, listening for any conformation of what he was hearing. The colonel closed his eye for a long moment dosing off into a twilight sleep.

Date: December 23rd - Time: 4:45 AM

"Henry! Henry, wake up! You're having a nightmare!"

Jessup sat up, shaking. His body was soaked with perspiration. His hands trembling. His breathing racing. He was having another panic attack.

"You were back in that damned war again, weren't you? I think it's time you see the doctor again, get some stronger meds or something."

"I'm fine! Go back to sleep. It was just the accident last night. I'll be okay." But Jessup knew that was a lie. The PTS was back. The sight of the boy was burning in his head. The look of despair on the lieutenant's face and the sound of that round had exploded, again.

Time: 5.00 AM

The evening had been uneventful for the most part. That didn't upset Lemos in the least. This twelve-hour shift rotation made for a long night, but the three days off where nice. He sat quietly in his squad car at the front gate of the impound lot, mulling over what the sheriff had said. He felt pleased. It had been a good night.

He needed to check the lock before heading in. Andy had forgotten twice this month to lock it.

Opening the car door, a gust of wind sent a shiver through Lemos' body. "Burr, damn it's cold out here." He looked up. A solitary drop of rain grazed his cheek, bringing back the misery of the night before. "Rain in the air too. Hope it doesn't storm again like last night."

His thoughts were interrupted by a low growl. Lemos squatted down. "Well, hello, Duke! Taking care of things? Hey boy, what you got there?" He was answered with another low growl. "Come on, don't be worried, I'm not going to take it.

My mama didn't raise no fools." He watched the dog's tail waging while Duke still murmured in a low growl. "Looks like you found a shoe, but the heels missing, you chew it off?" *A pretty nice one at that*, he thought. He smiled at the old dog, saying, "You take care of things, I've got to get back to work." He stood up from petting the dog through the fence. When he got back to his car, Lemos shouted, "Go find the other one, it'll make your teeth stronger." And thought, *Maybe it'll help your breath too*.

Chapter 11

The Lifeline

Date: Unknown - Time: Daylight

Splat! Yates felt a cold drop hit the back of his left hand. His surroundings were more visible now. It was lighter. The endless darkness of night was ending. The sound of raindrops on metal. He looked up at the tiny hole for a beam of light. A ray of sunshine. It wasn't light enough to see yet. Wait! Maybe! He told himself. Yates strained his eye, trying to focus on the small opening. Yes, it was there. It was very faint, but the light was there. It was cloudy and raining. Another drop hit his little finger. "Raining! Yes, water!" he shouted.

His eye searched frantically for its source, to find a reservoir. Bill moved his hand to feel around like he'd done before. *Come on, be there*, he pleaded.

"To the right, a little further is where you felt it before," his mentor commanded.

He felt two or three more drops hit the back of his hand. Yes, it was still dripping. A small tear formed in the corner of his eye. Rampant desire overtook his logic. He had to get the rain before it stopped dripping.

Yates turned his palm up and moved it to the right, trying to cup the water. His shoulder was throbbing in an agonizing dull pain, making him sick to his stomach as he tried to reach his mouth. He felt the water seeping into the crevices of his palm and running up his arm. The rain was overflowing in his palm. He was losing this vital lifeline. Bill couldn't bring his hand up to quench his thrust. He realized the burning in his eye had stopped.

"Open your right eye. Maybe you can now. Come on, open your eye, Yates!"

It wouldn't open. He could feel nothing in his eye. It was no use.

"Look up, can you see anything yet?"

It was getting lighter now. It must be getting daylight out. *Okay, think...*

He pulled his right hand over his body very carefully and poured it into his left hand. Then brought his free hand up along his stomach and chest while bringing his chin down as low as possible. Bill's wet palm touched his bottom lip, causing a few drops to spill into his mouth. He licked off his wet hand to take in every bit of moisture. *Good*, he thought, *but not enough. I need more.*

"Be patient, Bill. Rest, the light of day will be here soon."

Yates closed his eye relaxing... *The water is so peaceful this evening. It just reaches up to meet the sky. The sky is so blue. The hovering clouds of silvery gray are lined in pink. "Red sky at night, sailors' delight." The sand is so soft and warm on the serene beach. The clouds are billowing and beginning to thicken and gather. There are dark skies on the horizon. A storm is coming. "Red sky in the morning, sailors take warning." Thunder - yes, the rain will come soo...*

CRASH! A loud clap of thunder jolted Yates back to reality. Through the wind, he could hear the rain beating the metal above him. Beneath him, the water was collecting in a small puddle. Then he heard the sound of voices coming from his blind side. It was the last voice he heard from the day before.

"Set it down over there, Mike. I'll take care of it later, when the rain lets up."

A younger voice replied, "Will you unhook the safety chain on that side, Andy?"

So that's his name, Bill thought. "Help! Please help me!" But his cry for help was drowned out by the other sounds clamoring around him.

"Where'd you pick this one up, Mike?"

The person named Mike didn't answering the question, but replied instead, "The delivery ticket is on the seat."

Bill could hear a door open and a reply. "Oh yeah, I'll get it, Mike."

"Well I'm glad that one's done. Did you sign the ticket? I've got to run. Got one more to pick up before lunch, and it's all the way on the other side of the county."

"Sure, Mike, everything all signed, sealed and delivered."

The guy named Mike thanked Andy for his help. While slamming the door closed, he shouted, "Give Duke a big kiss for me. I'll take a minute to play with him the next time I come by."

Bill reflected, *So that's the name of that fucking mutt. Duke!*

He listened to Andy's laughing response. "That slobbering old mutt, hell I'd rather kiss your toothless sister." He heard the engine start up and then the sound of the vehicle pulling away. The voices and sounds dwindled to silence again.

They've gone, he resolved. *No use anymore. No one can hear me, no one cares...*(No man is an island). *I am an island. Am I an island Lord? Do I exist? Am I really here? Is this my eternal hell?*

What have I done to deserve this living hell? If this is to be my place in hell, then let it be. I'm too tired to fight it. Too cold, too weak. I can feel my intestines closing. The pain is sickening. My back burns with hot steel rod. My fingers will no longer move. The little beam of light, my tiny ray of hope exists no more. All options are gone. Release me, God, from this agonizing bondage.

"There are very few circumstances in life that can overshadow the will to live. Oh sure, most of us have contemplated it to some degree at one time or another. Like, for instance, total denial of oneself is - suicide. Giving one's own life for the life of another is - love. A belief so strong you sacrifice your life is - faith. But to contemplate death because you feel trapped - claustrophobic. I cannot accept giving up for that! Your will to live is no exception, Yates. It is instinctive. It is the strongest of all the emotions. A feeling that grasps for the

faintest glimmer of light at the end of the tunnel. There are other options. If you are to regain control and freedom again, you must accept your limitations. Focus on the mission. DON'T FAIL AGAIN! Blot out the pain, the fears, the cold. Concentrate and focus. You do that, then maybe you can get out of this cluster fuck."

"I have no dominion over my body anymore. My ability to think rationally weakens with every breath. You were my only salvation." Bill felt a warmth come over his body and he felt clean...with a fresh wet feeling on his hand. The sound of water spilling slow and steady. That refreshing sound… "Dripping Sound!" *Where is it? Look! Focus!* he told himself.

Searching his range of vision he spotted something in the dark shadows of the twisted metal above him. Bill told himself to concentrate on that spot. It was to the right, about a foot away. Without depth perception that was only a guess-timation, but water was pooling up there. He attacked in desperation across his body. Sharp pain ripped through his shoulder, causing him to instantly recoil in retreat. *I need to concentrate.* He reached up again, directing his moves, but again he was forced to relax in despair.

"Reach over there - again! Don't give up. You need that water," commanded his mentor.

The colonel, with renewed determination, forced his arm upward across his body, straining so hard his pulse throbbed in his temples. He was again forced to retreat. It was no use. His reach was two or three inches short of its destination.

"Okay, clear your mind. Concentrate on the mission, Colonel, Improvise! Isn't that what a Marine does? When the plan falls short, you don't quit, you improvise!"

Bill tried to think, clear his mind, as he'd been directed to do. Look for something, anything, any way possible. He needed that water. Some wires came into view from the shadows over his head to the left. It was too dark to see what was up there.

Reaching up over his head with his left hand, fighting the stabbing pain, he grabbed the wires and yanked as hard as he could. Bill heard a loud snap and suddenly it came down on his face. The yank on the wires shot deep into his left shoulder, but there was no time to dwell on the pain. He pulled the tangled conglomeration off his face and neck, trying to see what was there. A hose, tubing, maybe something to use as a channel. He felt something other than the wires. What was it? Yates tried to bring it over his head to see what it was, but he couldn't. It was still attached above. He touched it with his fingers; it was round and rubbery. Rubber tubing, that was it. He pulled as hard as he could to break it loose. "Break free damn it!" Snap! It lashed over his head, hitting his face. "Oh God, let it be long enough," He murmured. "Light, I need more light."

He felt it with his trembling fingers, directing himself not to drop it. He looked back over his chest to the left where the water was pooling. Laying the tube on his chest, he reached down and flipped the tip into the reservoir. It fell out, too flexible. He needed something to keep it rigid. He remembered the piece of wood on the ground from when he was first able to eye again. He felt around below him, being careful not to lose the tubing. His hand touched something cold. It was flat, about a quarter-inch thick, sticking up from the ground. It came out without resistance. It was about eight or nine inches long and narrowed at one end. *Yes, it may work*, he thought. Turning it in his hand so that the narrow end was toward him, he slipped it under the flexible tubing. Yates guided the tool, while holding on to both so it won't slip off to the edge of the pool. Then he pushed the tip into the water. *Hold it tight,* he told himself as he pulled his head down so his chin was resting on his chest. *That's it!*

Almost instantly the sparkling gift of God was dripping out of the small tube. Bill lifted it to his mouth and sucked it in. He began coughing and chocking.

"Not so fast, don't waste it, Yates!"

It hurt to swallow, but it was a bittersweet pain. He needed to swallow. With the pain would come strength. Bill, pleased with himself, conjectured, *Water. The second most needed lifeline to sustain life... To sustain my life....,a while longer.* He relaxed his head and drew back the tubing, lying it on his chest, falling off into dreamland.

PART II

NO TIME TO LOSE

Chapter 12

Questions But No Answers

Date: December 23rd - Time: 7:15 AM

Sheriff Marshall spotted Lemos walking from the corridor to the street. He jumped from his chair and rounded his desk in a hurry, heading for the door. "Bob, hey, Lemos, can I speak to you a moment?"

Bob turned just short of the door thinking, *Damn just not quick enough.*

Lemos smiled at the sheriff and walked back through the doorway of the sheriff's office. "Sure, Dave, what is it?"

Marshall placed a hand on Bob's shoulder as they went back into his office. "Glad I caught you before you left. Have a rough time out there last night?"

"No, not really, it's just this twelve-hour rotation gets to me after a few days. But I like the extra days off. What is it you wanted, sir?" Lemos followed Marshall back to his desk and took a seat. The sheriff rounded his desk and sat down.

"I had Knapp do some checking on that fancy caddy you had towed in yesterday."

"You did? Jub didn't say anything about it at the shift change this morning or before my shift last night. What'd he find out?"

The sheriff leaning back in his chair.

"Nothing. Not a trace. It seems that Mr. Yates has just disappeared. Knapp checked all of the residences in the area where you found the vehicle and no one has seem him. We also check all of the motels in the area and got zilch. I had Jub call the last known phone number we got off the DMV report. He got a message machine with one of those commercially produced messages. Knapp left a message for anyone to call us back as soon as they returned."

"What do you make of it, Dave?"

Marshall shrugged his shoulders. "I was going to ask you the same question."

Bob held up a manila envelope he was carrying. "Frank Rocha sent over a copy of the property report. I haven't had time to look at it yet; I just got it out of my message box this morning. If you'd like, sir, we could take a look at it now to see if there's anything in it that would make sense of all this."

"No, it's probably nothing. I just wanted to let you know what we found. He'll no doubt show up today sometime wanting to know why we impounded his expensive toy. No, You have a nice Christmas and we'll see you on Monday."

Bob got up and walked to the door. "I'll fill you in if I see anything in the report."

The sheriff's face supported an unsure expression, seemingly in deep thought, but he smiled, replying, "What? Oh – Okay, Bob, See you Monday."

Time: 8:25 AM

Bob stood in front of the microwave, nuking a cup of yesterday's coffee. His mind had drifted back, questioning the unsure look on Marshall's face when the buzzer sounded and the cup stopped turning. He took the cup out, added creamer, then went back to the kitchen table and sat down. The night had been a quiet one and that was good, but it made the time drag by, and that was bad.

Lifting the little metal tab on the envelope and taking a sip of bitter coffee, Bob pulled out the property report and emptied the other contents on the table. The property report was verbatim to what Frank had told him yesterday afternoon. The five Polaroids were also there. They was one picture with three people that looked to be on vacation, two pictures of a young boy, one of a nice-looking woman in walking shorts and one of a man, also in shorts. This must be Mr. Yates and his family. There were names and dates on the backs; Joey, Bill and Beth - Christmas 1997, Joey at lost pines - 1998, Joe - summer of 1998, Bill at Lost Pines - 1998, Beth at Lost Pines - 1998. They'd been taken nine years ago.

Bob looked at the DMV report: William R. Yates, 12671 Fairway Drive, San Antonio, Texas. AAA auto insurance and no points, not even so much as a parking ticket. This guy is an upstanding citizen from an upper-class community in San Antonio, Texas. He drove a classy American-made sports car worth over ninety thousand, with vanity plates 'RU-BULY-2'. He carried pictures taken over nine years ago, had ten bottles of booze in his trunk and two suitcases. He'd been drinking in the car and the bottle of liquor had spilled out on the seat.

Lemos wondered what this guy was running from, or trying to get away from. Where was he going on a night like that? Where was he coming from? He felt something else in the envelope, reached in, and pulled out the cap from the bottle of booze. He left the contents lying on the kitchen table, heading for the bedroom. He couldn't make head nor tail of what he'd seen. There where a lot of questions with no answers. It was time to call it a night, or was it a day? he wondered, then sighed. "This damned twelve-hour shit is about to kill me," and he flopped across the bed.

Chapter 13

Mrs. Romalez

Date: December 23rd - Time: 11:10 AM

Lemos was startled from a dreamless sleep by the ringing of the telephone. He realized he hadn't even undressed or gotten into bed. He picked up the receiver from the phone on the nightstand. "Hello?"

The voice on the other end was the dayshift dispatch, Susan McNally.

"Hello, Bob, Deputy McNally here. Sorry to bother you. Did I wake you?"

He squinted at the clock on the stand. It was 11:13 and he wondered if it was day or night. He glanced at the window. It was light out.

"That's okay, Susan, what's up?"

"Gee, I'm sorry, Bob. You're on that new twelve-hour shift rotation they're trying, aren't you?"

"Yeah, but I've got three days off now. I don't have to be back until Monday at 5:45 a.m." Yawning, "What can I do for you?"

"I wouldn't have bothered you, but Under Sheriff Knapp thought, under the circumstances, we had better give you a call."

Lemos sat up on the edge of the bed. "What circumstances?"

"Mrs. Romalez is here and she wants to speak to you, personally."

"Who?"

"You know, about her brother and sister-in-law, in the accident out on 41st Street the other day."

"Oh yes." He remembered something about a sister of the man that was killed. "What does she want from me?"

"She says she wants to thank you herself and tell you that Felippa and her sister-in-law never drank."

Bob, still trying to wake up, was confused. "Never drank? There was no mention of alcohol from the coroner's report. What's that all about?"

"I don't know, Bob, but she's obviously very concerned."

He looked at the clock, yawned again and said, "All right, it's 11:15. I can be there by noon."

"Fine, by noon then. I'll tell her and I'm sorry I had to wake you."

Lemos assure the dispatch that it was okay and hung up the phone. He undressed, grabbed a clean pair of shorts out of the dresser, yawning all the way to the bathroom, "Damn, I can't get used to these hours," and hit the shower.

Lemos entered the station. The row of chairs along the wall was filled. Four young boys and a girl occupied the first five. A woman with a blue scarf covering her hair was on the end. Bob knew that was Mrs. Romalez. He walked over to the window at the front counter. McNally looked up, smiled and nodded toward the lady in the scarf. Lemos turned and waked over to the row of metal chairs that lined the wall. The teens didn't look like locals. They appeared to be a group of punkers.

Mrs. Romalez was a large but pleasant-looking woman in her mid to late thirties. Her clothes were plain, clean and neat. She had a flawless dark complexion and long black hair that hung over her shoulders under the blue scarf. On her arm was a large cloth handbag that matched her scarf. It appeared to be handcrafted. She had a gentle mannerism that radiated, even before they spoke. Bob could tell she was deeply grieved by the circumstances and was in mourning.

"Hello, Mrs. Romalez, I'm Deputy Sergeant Lemos."

She looked up, forcing a smile. "Oh Gracias Señor Lemes for taking time from your busy day to see me."

Lemos reached down and took her hand to help the lady to her feet. "I'm so sorry for your loss, ma'am." Then pointing to the door at the opposite end of the metal chairs, "Why don't we step in there, Mrs. Romalez? It will be much quieter for us to talk."

As they passed by the teens to go into the room, one of the boys stuck out his feet, obviously attempting to force them to go around. Bob, just as obviously, kicked the boy accidentally just above the ankle saying, "Oh Gosh! Sorry about that, son. I didn't see you lying there."

The young punker countered in a cocky tone, "I ain't your son."

Lemos stopped, leaned down close to the kids and looked into the young man's eyes. "Oh, excuse me. I didn't mean my 'son', or the 'sun' in the sky. I meant 'Son of a Bitch!' Now, get your fucking feet out of the isle before I break your ankle!"

The punker sat up in his chair, glaring at Lemos, smirking in defiance while the others giggled and taunted him. Bob stood up, smiled and continued into the room.

Lemos pointed at the chairs around the table in the center of the room. "Have a seat, Mrs. Romalez." They both sat down.

"How can I help you? How is the little girl doing?"

Mrs. Romalez smiled broadly. "Emilia, she will be fine, thank you. I want to tell you yo mismo. Ah, veamos, myself." She began to cry. "Muchas gracias for trying to help my...Felippa and...and Maria...and saving Emilia. This is such a bad thing that has happened."

Bob placed his hand on hers and squeezed gently. "Yes, it is, ma'am. I wish we could have done more."

"I know you do your best, Señor Lemes. My heart is very sad about this bad thing that has happened. I have prayed to God and the Holy Mother to give them peace. I told the Lord to tell them that we will care for little Emilia the way my Felippa and Maria would have me."

"I'm sure Emilia will be taken care of very well, Mrs. Romalez. Do you have any other children?"

Her eyes lit up and a smile appeared, "Si, how you say...nueve muchachos."

"Nine boys?"

"We are very happy to have Emilia come into our family. We always wanted a baby girl."

Lemos raised his eyebrows, leaned back in his chair and replied, "Yes, yah, I suppose so," while thinking, *I pity the poor bastard who tries getting close to this girl in about fifteen years.*

"Ma'am, Deputy McNally, the lady at the front counter, said that you are worried about your brother drinking? You don't need to be concerned about anything..."

"No! ¡De ningún modo!" She was shaking her head and waving her finger back and forth. "Felippa would never drink. He was very close to the Lord and the Virgin Mother."

Lemos was surprised how adamant she was. "Why are you so concerned, Mrs. Romalez? There was nothing found to indicate that alcohol contributed to the accident."

She retorted in a stern voice; "The Police man that gave me Felippa's, how you say, cosas? Ah stuff."

"His personal property."

"Si, his...his stuff from the car. He put a...a Tequila, you know...ah liquor bottle in there too. Felippa would never take drink. Too close to Jesus and the Holy Mother. This is not right. I tell you something is wrong, Officer Lemes. This not Felippa's. He is too close to the Lord and the Holy Mother."

Lemos tried to calm the lady, saying, "I'm sure there's some mix up that we can get straightened out. You don't need to worry about it. Besides we don't have anything that would indicate there was any liquor in the vehicle."

Mrs. Romalez stopped, looked Lemos in the eyes, then reached into her blue handbag and took out a plastic bag containing several items. She opened the plastic bag and withdrew the remains of a broken bottle, which she laid on the table.

Lemos waited, expected to see more come out of her handbag, but that was it.

He looked up. "What. This is it? The neck of a...a liquor bottle."

"Si! And it is not Felippa's. He is to close to..."

"Yes, I know, ma'am, but I thought you had more." The woman slowly shook her head in an unsure manner.

"No, just thes, and the book."

"What book, ma'am?"

"The Englo book, *Cuento corto*."

"Where is the book now, Mrs. Romalez?"

With a flippant gesture she answered, "I gave it to the man at the garage. I do not read such things, and I know Felippa would not read this either."

"Maybe it was Marie's book, she was American, wasn't she?"

"Si, her papa was American, from the city of Chicago, but Marie never know her papa. Just her mama raised her. She would not read this book either, only the Bible and her church magazines."

Lemos stood up and patted Mrs. Romalez's hand. "Please don't let this bother you. The broken bottle top was probably lying on the table when they did the personal property report and was put in the bag by mistake.

There was a moment of silence as the two of them smiled at each other. Mrs. Romalez stood up slowly and offered her hand to the deputy saying, "I just wanted to thank you, Señor Lemes, for saving our little Emilia for us."

Bob grabbed her hand with both of his. "You're welcome, ma'am, have a safe trip back to Larado and a very Merry Christmas, Mrs. Romalez."

She looked at Bob with penetrating eyes. "I can tell you are a good man, Señor Bob, and Feliz Navidad to you and your loved ones." He could feel the warmth she generated releasing from his hand as she walked out the door.

Chapter 14

Bingo!

Date: December 23rd - Time: 1:00 PM

Bob shed his cloths and crawled slowly between the cool sheets, letting them massage every fiber of his weary body. At that moment he felt he could stay there forever and never get up. He sighed, falling asleep almost before his head hit the pillow.

"HOLY SHIT! That's it!" His eyes bugging wide while turning to look at the clock on the nightstand. 1:20 p.m. He threw back the covers sitting up in one quick motion, thinking, No time to lose. Bob pulled on his pants, stepped into his shoes and grabbed his shirt. He darted into the kitchen and there it was, on the table where he'd left it.

Bob reached down, picked up the bottle top with the partial liquor control band lying next to the pictures and was out the front door of his apartment in seconds. *Why didn't I think of it before?* he scolded. He got into his car, started it and barreled around the corner from the apartment. "I hope I'm not too late. Damn! Why didn't I think of it?"

Lemos pulled up in the no-parking area in front of the office, jumped out of the car taking the five steps to the entrance in two leaps.

He bolted past the front counter without saying a word. He saw the dispatcher talking on the phone and headed directly into the interrogation room, hoping to see what he'd come for. The table was bare; he spotted a wastebasket and reached in. There it was, the broken bottle. The neck of a liquor bottle. He looked at the broken piece of glass. The control stamp was still intact. Bob reached into his pocket for the partial liquor control band he'd grabbed off his kitchen table and read it. '355M06'. Then he took out the one that was in the wastebasket. The band wrapped across the top and down both sides of the bottleneck in his hand. The bottle hadn't been opened. 'TLCC758356M06'. BINGO!

Chapter 15

The Lost Pines

Date and time: Unknown

"Bill! Bill? William R. Yates, are you in there? Come see, he just did it. Look, honey, he's doing it again." Bill peaked through the screen of the back door from the kitchen.

"See what, Beth?"

"Come out here, in the back yard. He just did it. He'll do it again. Okay, Joey, walk to Mommy. Come on, get up and walk to Mommy like a good boy."

He swung the screen door open. "Sure, Beth, I can tell. He'll probably be running in the Boston Marathon next month."

Beth pulled straight up on Joey's hands, trying frantically to get the boy to repeat his actions. Joey would have no part of it. He was more interested in a small ant he'd spotted on the steps to the back yard.

"Just watch for a minute, he'll do it again," she insisted. Then she continued; "Joey, stand up and walk to Daddy. I know you can."

"For Christ's sake, he's only ten months old, give him some time."

"I tell you he walked, Bill, and he isn't ten months, he's almost eleven. He took three steps the first time and two the second."

Beth looked at her husband standing in the doorway to the kitchen and smiled. "Honey, it's so nice out today, it seems a sin to waste it. Why don't we take a boat ride up the river? I don't want to just set here at the cabin all weekend. Lost Pines is beautiful this time of year. We haven't been out all winter. The blue bonnets are in full bloom now. The sky is so clear and blue you can almost swim in it. Come on, wha-do-ya-say? We could get ready and be on the river in less than an hour."

With a worried look and shaking his head, Bill replied, "I really can't take the time."

Beth persisted, "Take a deep breath, honey, I can smell the blue bonnets from he..."

He interrupted her. "I know what I smell. The shit I'm going to be in if I don't get those oil production reports to the Railroad Commission on time."

Beth stood up from the steps where she'd been sitting and walked up to her husband standing in the doorway. "Bill," she begged in a disappointed tone. "It's Saturday. You've been at the office every night this week until after ten. Please, give it a break. Give us a break. We need your attention too."

He stepped out on the back porch as Beth approached him seductively, and in a warm low breathy voice she said, "I thought maybe we could put Joey in his playpen, (She rubbed up against her husband), and after we take a shower together, (She reached down, unzipped his pants and reached inside), I will nibble on your..."

"Beth, take it easy." He recoiled. "It hurts when you squeeze so hard."

She continued relentlessly, teasing him saying, "Hard? Did I hear you say hard?"

He began to weaken, not backing off now in total disapproval, looking down at her.

"Elizabeth Wilson Yates, I've got too many things on my mind to...to do you any good. I...I think..."

Beth intensified her attack. "Do I feel something? Why yes, I believe I do. I think it's begriming to stand up and take notice. Could it be you're having second thoughts?"

Bill was pinned to the wall beside the kitchen door; his wife now pressed tightly against him and moving rhythmically.

"Hmm! That's funny, I suddenly feel like taking a shower. Why don't you put Joey in his playpen while I go up and get the water warm? Oh, you better change his diaper too, it smells like he needs it."

"Go on up, honey, I promise not to leave you hanging around long." He could hear her laughing as the screen door closed behind him.

Tiny goose bumps covered his shivering body. "Damn, this water's cold. Is there something wrong with the hot water heater?"

Beth's stimulating gentle touch to his chest and genitals was inhibited by the cold water running up his arm.

In a soft voice she commented, "It feels hot to me, Bill. Steamy hot."

His inadequacy angering him. "Beth, I'm never going to get it up in this cold."

In a throaty whisper she persisted, "I know what will get you up." Sinking to her knees she said, "A little nibble alwa..."

"Get up, Beth. It's not going to happen. I'm too damn cold! This fucking shower is like ice!"

His wife stood up, obviously dejected, throwing open the shower door. "It always ends the same, doesn't it, Bill? Different stories, different reasons, but with the same ending. Well, go fuck yourself, I don't need you!"

"Beth, Beth, honey, come back, it's just that the water's so cold. Come back - come back, please."

Bill stood trembling in the cold shower, squeezing his eyes so tight his head throbbed, in complete disgust with himself. When he opened them, there was his Beth. A feeling of renewed joy come over him. She had come back.

"I'll come back you, BASTARD! I'll come back and cut your fucking dick off."

"Beth! What are you doing! Put those scissors down!" Pain stabbed deep into his shoulder. "Christ, my shoulder. Beth, don't, my shoulder!" He could see her wheeling the scissors at his neck again. His body tensed in fear of the blow. He fought to block out the screaming.

"YOU bastard! You bastard! You bast..."

"Stop! Stop Damn it! Oh, Christ, my shoulder!"

"Wait, Bill, Clear out the cobwebs."

Bill wondered what time it was. Was it still day or was it night again? The tiny hole above him wasn't sending its gleaming rays of sunshine across its stage of twisted metal. He turned his head to look at the ground. The water was pooling beneath him, and then he realized, the sound of the drops hitting the metal above him. It was daytime and raining again. Bill looked back at the hole to his left, but he couldn't tell how close it was to darkness with out its illuminating rays.

"The water, Yates, you need the water!"

Water! Yes, he thought. *I need to get more water.* Anxiety took control. *Where is my tube, my tool? Think, Bill, think,* he told himself.

Franticly the colonel looked around not knowing where it was. He looked back to the ground, worried that he'd dropped it. Then he remembered, reaching just inside the collar of his coat, there it was. As he pulled out the small piece of wood and tubing, his eye scanned the twisted metal for the reservoir. It was dripping slowly above to the left. He could feel the lesions in his throat from being so dry, knowing it meant pain and lots of it. But he had to get the water into his mouth. His hands were so cold. The aching in his fingers caused uncontrollable shaking.

"You know the routine, Marine! Now do it. The trembling stopped you before. The mission could have been compromised, and many lives were at stake. You knew what you had to do. You could not overcome that fear; the agonizing knowledge that there was no other option. Don't fail your mission!"

Yates guided the stick up then pushed the tubing into the pool as before. It began to drip almost immediately. *Oh, sweet wet,* he thought, resisting the pain to swallow. He needed to drown out the fire in his throat. *I'm so thirsty, so cold, so sleep...* Bill's trembling hand dropped and the tubing fell to the ground as dazzling colors danced from his mind into darkness.

Chapter 16

No Time To Lose

Date: December 23rd - Time: 1:45 PM

Deputy Lemos headed for the front counter. The two office workers were busy doing paperwork. McNally was still talking on the private line for outgoing calls. She never raised her head. There were two people sitting in the metal chairs along the wall. Bob turned back down the corridor to the sheriff's office. The door was open, but no one was there. He turned quickly down the hall into the deputy's bay. The sheriff wasn't there either. Bob retreated back to the front counter.

The thought kept pounding in his head about a connection; there had to be a connection. Deputy McNally was still talking on the private line, smiling at something that was said. The other workers didn't look up. There was no time to wait. He needed to find the sheriff, and find him now.

"Susan! Have you seen the sheriff? He's not in his office."

Irritated by the intrusion, the dispatcher frowned while pointing at the receiver in her hand and kept talking.

"I need to talk to the sheriff."

Puckering her lips in a disgusted why, McNally retorted; "Hold your horses there, Deputy, I'm on the phone."

BANG! Bob slammed his hand down hard on the counter, startling everyone in the room to attention.

"Damn it, Susan, this is more important than your personal calls. I need to talk with Sheriff Marshall, now!"

Embarrassed by Bob's reaction, McNally laid the receiver down saying, "Hang on a sec, honey, we've got an irate deputy here about to split a gut. Yes, Bob, what is it?"

"I need to speak with the sheriff, it's important that I talk with him now."

"I thought you were off for the next three days."

"Yes, yes, but where is the sheriff? Is he in the building?"

"No. He's with the County Commissioner."

"Is Jub Knapp in then?"

"No, he's with the sheriff. He said they'd be back around four."

Bob retorted, "That's too long!" Lemos bolted toward the front entrance ordering McNally to call the Commissioner's office and find the sheriff. He was on his way there and it was urgent he spoke to him.

He heard the dispatcher in the background saying, "What's the big hurry, he'll be back in a couple of hours."

Lemos responded as he charged through the door, "Just do it!"

Time - 2:00 PM

Lemos entered the reception area of the commissioner's officer. The new County facilities, located in Paw Paw, were an excellent example of the public's tax dollars at work. Commissioner Davis' office was no exception. The room was larger than Bob's entire apartment and luxuriously decorated.

Bob walked across the room to the receptionist, who was leafing through a McCall. He mused that the artificial plant in the corner of the waiting area probably cost more than all of his furnishings put together. It was a depressing reminder of where his place was in the whole scheme of thing. He blocked out his disgusted feelings about the lavish decor. There was no time for it.

It was obvious McNally's search for the sheriff hadn't made it this far, at least not yet. The nameplate on the desk read 'Catherine Taylor'.

"Miss…Miss Taylor, excuse me please."

A bright round face, hallowed in silky long black hair that hung down over her shoulders, came up from the magazine, supporting a pleasant smile.

"Yes, may I help you?"

"Yes. Is Sheriff Marshall in with Commissioner Davis? I need to speak with him."

"Is he expecting you?"

"No, but it is important that I see him right away."

The receptionist, in a soft tone replied, "They're not taking any calls right now, but I can let the Commissioner's personal assistant know you're here. Who should I say is here to see him?"

"Ah…Oh, Lemos, Miss, Deputy Bob Lemos and please tell him it's urgent."

Miss Taylor stood up and scampered over to a set of double doors to her right and disappeared. He couldn't keep from perusing Miss Taylor's robust body, wondering how long she'd been tucked away up here for only the elite to admire.

He looked at his watch when the sheriff came through the double doors. Ten minutes had passed since he'd entered the Commissioner's office. Lemos recognized the frustrated look on Marshall's face as he approached.

"This had better be good, Bob. We're in the middle of a budget meeting, and I sure as hell don't want it to fall on my shoulders if it doesn't get done on time."

"Dave! There's a connection between Yates and the Lopez accident." Marshall looked at his watch, still preoccupied with the interruption to the meeting with Commissioner Davis.

"What gives you that idea? Aren't you supposed to be off the next three...?"

Bob cut the sheriff off. "Forget about that, sir. There's no time to lose. I've found something that puts Mr. Yates and the Lopez family together sometime before the accident."

"The abandoned caddy on M-40 and the accident on 41st Street? Well, come on, what is it?"

"The liquor control bands are consecutively numbered!"

"What on earth are you talking about, Lemos?"

"Sheriff, remember this morning at the end of my shift. We

were talking about the abandoned Cadillac. I told you that Frank from the garage had sent me a copy of the property report. I hadn't looked at it yet, but when I got to my place, I opened the envelope. With the report, he included some pictures. Stuck in there with the pictures and the report was part of a control band from a liquor bottle. It must have been lying on the seat of Yates' car or something."

"So how does that connect to the accident, Bob? The Cadillac was on M-40, wasn't it?"

"Mr. Lopez's sister - Mrs. Romalez, sir. She came into the office at noon. She wanted to thank us for saving the child and trying to help her brother and sister-in-law."

"Yes. The lady that took custody of the child. She wanted to talk to you personally. I told Knapp that you were off for a few days and to take care of it."

"Anyway, I came in and spoke with her for a few minutes. She was quite grieved by the whole thing, plus she wanted to make it crystal clear that her brother didn't drink."

"Why was she concerned about that? There wasn't anything in the coroner's report that indicated alcohol contributed to the accident."

"I know, sir, I asked Mrs. Romalez the same question. I tried to convince her there was no need to worry. But after listening to her plead her brother Felippa's religious convictions for several minutes, she pulled out of her handbag the neck of a broken whiskey bottle that was found in the Lopez car. I didn't think anything about it then. In fact, I told Mrs. Romalez it was probably just lying on the table when they made out the property report and got put with her brother belongings by mistake.

"When I got home, it hit me to check the control number of the broken bottle and the partial stuck in with the report and pictures sent over from the County garage. The last five numbers of the band in Yates' caddy are consecutive with the one Mrs. Romalez gave me. That bottle hadn't been opened and the control band was still sealing the bottle cap. Sheriff, I'm convinced that Mr. Yates was in the Lopez car."

"It does put them together, doesn't it?"

"Sir, without a doubt. Yates was in the Lopez car before the accident and I think our Mr. Yates is out there somewhere yet. Or worse, he could have been in the car during the accident. Maybe he wandered off or was thrown from the vehicle and is lying at the bottom of the gorge injured or dead."

Marshall snapped, "We need to organize a search. Go back to the office. Have McNally and the admin staff get a hold of the off shift. Also, have them call the fire departments in the area for volunteers, along with the civil defense volunteers." He turned to go back into the Commissioner's office saying, "That'll give me some time to brief Knapp and Commissioner Davis on the situation."

Lemos started for the outer door of the office, but before he could take a step a hand landed on his shoulder.

"A nice piece of detective work, Bob." Marshall looked at his watch. "It's 2:20 now. I want the team leaders of the search parties in the training room by 3:30. Now go! NO TIME TO LOSE!"

Bob thought as he whipped open the door to leave, *That's what I was trying to tell you.*

Chapter 17

The Meeting

Date: December 23rd - Time: 3:35 PM

Six individuals where gathered around a large table in the front of the training room. The sheriff was sitting at the head of the table. Next to him was The Under Sheriff Jub Knapp, then Deputy Bob Lemos. On the opposite side, next to Dave Marshall was Nick Taylor, Chief of the Paw Paw Fire Department, and then Pete Duffy from the civil defense team. Seated by the wall next to the County map was Deputy Kin Kinnopplus.

The sheriff thanked them all for coming on such short notice. Then he asked Deputy Lemos to fill everyone in on why they were asking for help in the search.

Bob began by saying, "The sheriff and I have reason to believe that a Mr. William R. Yates is somewhere in the area of Three Mile Lake. You can see the area on the map that we are concerned with. It's about a three-mile area that runs along the ravine on 41st Street South to 62nd Avenue and North of Paw Paw Road."

Pete Duffy asked why we felt this man was out there in the first place. Bob explained to the group in a shortened version that he became suspicious of the situation after finding Mr. Yates' ninety-thousand-dollar vehicle abandoned with the key still in the ignition the night of the ice storm. Then needing to have it towed so the County road crews wouldn't hit it. Plus the fact it hadn't been claimed now for three days. He also told them they had found a connection between Mr. Yates and the

Lopez accident, but he didn't mention what the connection was.

Everyone knew about the double fatality via the media coverage. Chief Taylor asked if there had been a missing person's report filed by anyone. Lemos told them there had not, but after checking the motels in the area and the residences on 41st Street in the area, plus not being able to reach anyone from the last known address, the decision was made to form a search party. He added, "It is very possible Mr. Yates was in the vehicle during the accident and either got out or was thrown out."

Jub Knapp suggested a central command be set up at the impound lot. It was only about five miles from where the crash occurred and had the largest area for parking the volunteers' vehicles. The office also has a radio transmitter for contacting County vehicles.

The sheriff stood up, saying as he walked over to the County map and pointed at the location of the accident, "I know it's late in the day and we're going to be working into the night, but you're all aware if Yates is out there, every second could be the difference of whether we find him alive or not."

The sheriff told Kin to have the dispatch contact whoever it was in charge at the impound lot. Kinnopplus replied, "That would be Andy Sharpe, sir," as he got up to leave the room.

"Good. We will be using his office as our command center." Then he turned back to the map. "We will concentrate our search in this area. Chief Taylor, I would like your men and the civil defense volunteers to conduct the ground search in this two-mile area on 41st Street North to M-40 and South to Paw Paw Road. It'll be rough going along the ravine and in this wooded area south, but I think your guys are the best qualified if we do find Yates alive."

With that the Chief stood up. "We're on it, Dave." Pete Duffy followed the fire chief out the door.

Marshall continued, "Jub, you and the off shift start a house to house from where you checked yesterday. Continue five miles north and south on 41st Street and five miles east and west on 62nd Avenue and north of Paw Paw Road." The sheriff walked back to where Lemos was still setting.

"Bob, what EMS company was used at the Lopez accident?"

"Thompson's, Sheriff."

Marshall just stood there thinking for a moment, then asked, "What do you think about getting input on this from the paramedics that were the first responders on the accident?"

"It can't hurt, Dave. One of them crawled around in the vehicle for quite a while. Maybe he saw something that could make a difference, especially with what we know now." Marshall heard what he wanted to hear.

"All right then, get hold of the paramedic that was in the car. Have him meet us out at the command center. I want his take on this."

Bob got up from the chair, leaving the sheriff alone to his thoughts in the training room and headed for the deputies' bay. It was empty. Lemos sat down at his desk rummaging hastily through papers, file baskets, and under Styrofoam cups for his copy of the accident report, realizing his desk was long overdue for a good cleaning. It had the number to Thompson Emergency Medical Service. There it was, under the telephone where he'd left it so he wouldn't forget where it was. He turned to the second page. Thompson's EMS, 77-MEDIC. He punched in the numbers and it rang.

"Thompson EMS, Jennifer Reed speaking."

"Hello, Ms. Reed, I need to speak with Henry Jessup please."

"I'm sorry, sir, but Mr. Jessup is not available at the moment. Is this an emergency?"

"Yes, well no, not a medical emergency, but I need to speak with him."

"Oh, well, like I said, he isn't available. Is there anyone else you would like to speak to?"

"Is his partner, ah... I think her name is Jackie, is she in.?"

"No, sir, she isn't available either, but I would be glad to assist you."

"Is there a number where Mr. Jessup can be reached? It's very important."

"I'm sorry, sir, but he is not scheduled to work today. He will be back on the twenty seve..."

"Ms. Reed, this is Deputy Lemos from the Van Buren Sheriff's Office. It's urgent I get hold of Mr. Jessup. You do have his home number or a cell number where he can be reached, right?"

"I'm not allowed to give that information out Deputy Lemos, it's company policy."

Bob's patience was wearing thin. "Then I need to speak to your supervisor or someone that has the authority to get me in touch with Paramedic Jessup. It is concerning the double fatality on 41st Street and it's imperative I talk to him."

After a quick moment of silence, she replied, "Well I'm not supposed to do this, but if you're from the sheriff's office, I guess it should be all right. Hang on a second, I'll look at the list."

Bob waited a long minute before he heard the receiver being picked up. Ms. Reed told him it was Jessup's home phone number, then recited it as Lemos wrote it down. He thanked her and hit the reset button. He stabbed in the numbers to Jessup's home phone and it began to ring. It rang four times, and he was getting more impatient with each ring. On the fifth ring it was answered. It wasn't the medic's voice. When Bob asked if Mr. Jessup was in, the male's voice on the other end questioned, "Who wants to know?"

"This is Deputy Sergeant Lemos from the sheriff's department. I need to speak with Paramedic Jessup."

"Hang on a second, I'll get him." Lemos overheard the voice on the other end saying as the receiver was being put down.

"It's a Deputy something or other with a deep voice. He said he needs to talk with you. What's that all about, Henry?"

"This is Henry Jessup."

"Jessup, Bob Lemos here. Sheriff Marshall asked me to call you. He'd like you to meet us at the County impound lot."

"What for? I'm off today, we've got other plans to..."

Lemos interrupted. "Look. I haven't the time to go into it now, but it is extremely important that you go out there NOW!

It's that fenced-in lot out on M-40."

Henry clarified, "The one just North of 64th Street?"

"Yes, that's it."

"Okay, Sarge. I'll be there ASAP!"

The deputy heard the other voice comment as he hung up the phone, "I guess this screws up our...click!"

Bob grinned thinking, *Poor little sweetie*, as he pushed the reset, saying, "It's not Sarge, it's Sergeant." He then hit the numbers to the impound yard.

It rang only once. "County Storage, Andy here."

"Andy, Bob Lemos. Just wanted to check..."

In an excited tone Sharpe blurted; "I'm way ahead ayah, Bob. Hell there must be fifty people out here. They've got Duke so riled up I couldn't leave him in the shed. Had to chain 'im up out on the lot."

"It sounds like it, I can hear him out there. Is the search underway yet? And what about the sheriff, is he there yet?"

"Chief Taylor and his men are leaving now, but Sheriff Marshall hasn't showed yet."

"Then you know what this is all about?"

"Most of it, I guess."

Bob told him he would be out directly and to let the sheriff know the paramedic would be there as soon as possible. He hung up the phone, grabbed his coat and parka out of his locker, and headed for the front door.

Chapter 18

Command Center

Date: December 23rd - Time: 4:15 PM

Lemos could hear Duke out back when he pulled into the yard; he was definitely unhappy with all the commotion. Andy was right about the response. He could hardly find a place to park.

The sheriff was approaching as he came through the door. "Bob, glad you're here, I just got here myself. I've got Susan back at the office getting a copy of Yates' picture from the Texas DMV. She's going to run copies and have someone bring them out. Knapp's going to need them more than we will on his house to house."

Bob looked around the room. "Looks like things are going good here, sir. I thought I'd join the ground search with Chief Taylor's men."

Dave shook his head no. "I'd rather you stay here and coordinate things."

"But, Dave, they can use all the bodies they can get."

"No," the sheriff insisted. "You need to oversee things here."

"But I thought I could do more out with the ground teams."

"Believe me, you'll do more good here, accessible. If we get any leads, they'll come here, and I want you available to act on them. This is your party."

There were still several volunteers milling around and Jub's off-shift team was waiting for the ID pictures to arrive. Bob sat down at the desk listening to the congestion in the room and the commotion Duke was putting up out back, thinking to himself, *I feel so damned helpless in here.*

Marshall looked up and spotted Chief Taylor coming through the door. He raised his hand as he walked away from the desk to flag the fire chief, shouting, "Nick, Chief Taylor - Are your men and the civil defense teams ready?"

The chief stopped and turned around to see the sheriff approaching. "They've already started, Dave. We've sectioned off the area starting at the accident site. Each team has been assigned a hundred-yard grid. If we don't turn up anything, we'll spread out from there."

"Have you got someone coordinating things out there, Nick?"

"I've got Eddy Doolittle, one of my assistant fire chiefs, overseeing things."

"Isn't he the one that's, shall we say, a little stubborn?"

Chief Taylor interjected. "He voices his own opinion on things, and he can be hardheaded at time, but he always gets the job done. He'll be fine."

"Good, Chief, you know your men best."

The sheriff directed his attention back to Lemos. "Bob, where's that medic we want to talk with? Did you get in touch with him?"

Bob looked up from desk and replied, "Yes, sir, said he'd be here as soon as possible."

"Well, he's late!" Dave said as he approached the desk.

"I got a hold of him at home, Dave. He lives in Dowagiac, so it may take a little longer to get here."

"I want to see him as…" His comment was interrupted by the ruckus the dog was still making. "Will someone shut that mutt up out there?"

Bob looked at Andy Sharpe, who was scowling at the sheriff. Andy could call Duke a mutt, but he took offense at anyone else doing it, especially when they meant it.

Bob asked, "Will you do something with Duke? He's annoying the sheriff."

Sharpe replied, glaring at the sheriff, "Yeah, well, he's annoying me. About the only thing I can do is let 'im run. I just thought with all the crap going on out here it was better to chain 'im up."

"No, it's okay, Andy, you can let him loose. We won't be going out back. He'll be fine."

When Andy opened the back door of the office, Duke began wagging his bobbed tail so hard his whole rump wiggled. He began to whine in a high-pitched bark, jumping up in excitement. All the commotion had him confused, and he didn't like it. Not one bit. But seeing his master made it all better. He knew if he fussed enough the Alfa would come and pay attention to him. His massive shoulders pulled on the chain with enough force to almost snap his tether. Andy patted his head and smiled, "I know, old boy, they got me riled up too."

Duke danced around and sat in front of him whining for Andy's affection, but being careful not to jump up on him, that was a no-no and meant a scolding. Andy freed his partner, and he headed for his favorite hole under the old station wagon. Andy watched him go, hollering; "Go on, dig some more for your treasure." Andy, amused by his old friend, shook his head and returned to the office with a sigh. "He sure does think he's got somethin' special out there."

Time: 4:35 PM

"Sheriff, this is Henry Jessup. He's the medic that was in the Lopez car. He got the child out. Henry, Sheriff Marshall."

Jessup looked up at Marshall and extended his hand saying, "I remember you at the accident, but things were pretty hectic that night. We didn't really meet."

The sheriff shook his hand. "Ah yes, it was, and slippery too. Jessup, Henry is it? When you were in the Lopez car, do you recall anything unusual, something you wouldn't expect to see?"

"Like I said, Sheriff, it was hectic. My attention was on getting the people out alive. I can't say as I remember anything other than a lot of glass and metal. There was an extreme amount of blood from the injuries sustained by Mrs. Lopez. She was a large woman and hit the windshield without any restraint. Mrs. Lopez must have been sitting very close to her husband. Of course, it's hard to say, Sheriff, as the car had been turned over on its wheels by the time I got there."

Marshall puffed up like a blowfish. The veins in his neck bulging, he stepped back, partly in disbelief and partly in anger. "What do you mean the car was back on its wheels before you got there?"

Jessup startled by the sheriff's tone. "Like I said, the car was back on its wheels before I checked the victims."

Marshall snapped, "Christ, who masterminded that fuck up? You were in charge out there, Bob, don't tell me it was your screw up!"

"No, actually, Dave, Tom Murphy was the first one on the scene. I took over when I got there as senior deputy."

Henry was apprehensive with the tone of questioning. "What are you asking, Sheriff?"

"Do you recall anything that would indicate someone else was in the vehicle during or after the accident?"

Jessup looked at Lemos, asking, "Is there something I'm missing in this conversation? When I crawled into the back seat, there were all those bags and magazines covering the baby."

"No, we're not saying that you did anything wrong, Henry, but we do think there was a fourth person in the car before or during the accident."

"So that's the reason for all of this commotion. I guess it's possible that someone could've been in the car."

The sheriff asked, "Bob, What was the estimated speed of the vehicle when it left the road?"

"It couldn't be determined. With all the ice on the roads, there weren't any skid marks. Based on the road conditions, probably less than forty. It would have gained some momentum if the brakes were locked before leaving the road, but decreased upon hitting the guardrail."

Jessup replied, "I doubt anyone could have crawled out of that mess and lived to tell about it."

The sheriff's gaze went back to Henry, "The girl did."

Marshall stuck out his hand to Jessup and thanked him for coming out. He stressed to Lemos the need for him to be there to take charge and let him know if anything came up. He left saying that he was going back to the office and have an up-close and personal conversation with Deputy Murphy and mumbling some about not wanting to be blamed for Tom's screw up.

Lemos asked Jessup if he could step out front with him for some fresh air. Bob liked this guy, even if he was as queer as a three-dollar bill.

Henry smiled at him saying, "You're not my type," and followed the deputy outside. Bob leaned on the chain-link fence that surrounded the yard.

"Can I ask you a question, Henry?"

"Sure, you can ask, but ask me no questions, I'll tell you no lies."

"I heard the guy on the phone before we hung up. He sounded a little pissed. I got the feeling he was questioning who was calling you. Believe me, he doesn't have to worry."

"Marty? He's always a little jealous. Has been for the ten years we've been together. I have straight friends, both men and women, and Marty doesn't like any of them."

"Well, how did you decide, or know, ah..."

"That I was gay? Hnnnn. How did you decide or know that you were straight?"

"Well...ah...that's how I feel. I don't get turned on by men, just women."

"All women?"

"No, not all women."

"Me neither. The truth is, most men don't do anything for me. Men in general are afraid their machismo is going to be in question if they admit they see sexual attributes in both sexes, but we all do to some degree. I'd be lying if I said I've never seen a woman that didn't look sexy to me. That's just the way it is I guess."

The wind had picked up and the sky was clearing. There was a nip in the air. They walked down along the fence. Bob pointed at the cars in the fenced-in lot. "See those cars out there?"

Jessup looked out at the cars on the lot, some with red tags and others with blue.

"Yeah, what about 'em?"

"The red-tagged ones are here waiting for an investigation or trial. The blue tags are vehicles that are unclaimed for over thirty days. They all have a story to tell. Most of them with bad endings."

"What about those three?" Henry asked, nodding toward three cars without any tags.

"They've been cleared to be recycled," Bob replied, thinking to himself, *We could be friends, straight friends of course.*

Henry's eyes scanned the lot, the woods to the north and road behind them. "You think this guy's out there someplace or are you just spinning your wheels?"

Lemos pointed through the fence. "I don't think the story's ended on that one yet. I know Yates was in it."

Henry looked in that direction, spotting the old wagon. Bob continued, "I have a sick feeling he's out there somewhere crying for help. I'm probably all wet. I hope I am."

"Hey, don't be so hard on yourself. This Yates guy could be sitting in front of a nice warm fireplace somewhere with his feet up, sucking down a cold one. Besides, if he is out there yet, he's most likely dead."

"I hope you're right, Henry. If he's out there, he's probably dead either from the accident or the weather we've been having."

Henry looked up at the sky. The clouds were developing a reddish tint in the setting sun. Andy Sharpe walked up, following their gaze at the sky and said, "That means it's going to be cold tonight. Those boys out on the ground search are gonna need a cup of hot coffee when they come in. I'll get some brewing."

Henry was watching the dog through the fence. "What's your dog digging up out there?"

Andy laughed. "Oh Duke, that flea-bitten old mutt. He

thinks he's got a treasure buried under that wagon. Been digging out there for three days now. I never know what he's going to come up with. The other day he found a shoe, a pretty nice one at that."

The three of them turned to head back to the office. Bob put his hands in his pockets.

"Yeah, we better go in too. Getting chilly out here," Henry commented as they walked through the door. "Yates hah, I once knew a Lieutenant Yates."

"Navy Lieutenant?" Bob questioned.

"No, Marine. A first lieutenant when I was in the gulf, back in '91."

Chapter 19

To The Victor Go The Spoils

Date: Unknown - Time: Dusk

*W*hy should I endure the pain? All strength was gone. *I no longer want to exist. To feel the cold, or to see the dark shadows of this tomb I'm in.* The light from the little hole was getting weaker. *Is my body returning to unconsciousness or is the night on its way? My ray of hope has forsaking me too. All that's left is the anguish - mental and physical anguish. It hasn't deserted me.* Yates wondered if he was still alive, or was this his eternal damnation? *I have evaded my foe long enough. He is all that is left in my world.*

"*Come on shithead. That's enough of this 'Woe with me' crap. You call yourself a Marine? Why, you wouldn't make a pimple on a good Marine's ass. I'm disappointed in you, thinking of quitting. Those kind of thoughts go over like a turd in the punchbowl.*"

"Oh God, make him leave me alone. I don't want to hear him anymore."

"*Well, He's not going to do that, Colonel. I'm here because of him.*"

"Bullshit, the Lord no longer hears my plea. Besides, you're a pushy, self-centered, foulmouthed bastard. You're not from the Lord!"

"*Why so, Bill? Do you understand French? German? Of course not. I speak the language you understand. I'm the voice in your head. Listen to that sound! Is that endless scraping the sound of Satan coming to claim his reward?*"

It was the clawing, snarling sounds. His adversary was back close to him now, closer, ever closer. He could see the hole on the ground getting bigger; the front feet of the predator were digging the entrance larger. Soon it would be large enough. As Bill watched, it was as if it were in slow motion. The light was getting dimmer, but it didn't matter anymore. "Come on, come on, sweet Satan. Come on, man's best friend. My best friend. You're no longer the enemy. You are the only positive in my world of negatives."

Bill could hear the sound of vehicles rolling on gravel. There were voices in the distance. Duke had quit digging, and he was gone again. He looked at the ground beneath him. The gray shadows that reflected off the ground were back. That meant it was night again and the endless cold was coming. He could hear barking again, closer now. "Ah yes, There you are, my worthy friend. You have returned to continue your quest." Bill reached toward the ground to where he had felt it before. His hand touched it. If he can break it free, he'd show the beast that he was just as determined as it. "Come loose, damn it. I need something to defend myself in battle."

The snarling was at the entrance. "I see your massive head." Yates pulled with all his strength screaming, "Come loose, damn it, break free. He's at the entrance. Here he comes. Yes, I've got it. 'To the victor go the spoils!'" He swung down harder at the beast's snarling jaws!

"Hit him with the club! Yes, now again, with the leg! The Leg? Oh God, it is - it's my leg!"

Chapter 20

The End

Date: December 24 – Time: 1:15 AM

B ob hesitated with the phone in his hand. Then he pushing the buttons. He hated to make the call. Partly because it meant failure, which wasn't something he accepted with grace. But mostly because he knew Bill Yates was out there somewhere.

The phone rang. It was picked up on the second ring. A sleepy voice answered, "Hello."

"Hello, Sheriff?"

The sheriff sat up from where he had fallen asleep on the couch. "Yes, Bob, have you found him?"

"No, Dave, we haven't."

"Well, I was hoping, but I was afraid that was going to be the case."

Bob responded as he tapped on the desk with a pencil. "The assistant fire chief, Eddy Doolittle, just reported in. His teams have searched the area but came up blank. Not even a single sign."

"What about Knapp, anything from him yet?"

"No, sir. His men finished about three hours ago. The assistant chief said that his men and the civil defense volunteers are willing to continue if we felt there was any hope, but he didn't think there was any need to go on any further. I tend to agree with him, Dave."

Dave conceded. "Yes, I agree. Wrap it up out there and send them all home. We'll take another look at our options in the morning."

Bob sighed. "I just know that Mr. Yates is out there somewhere pleading for help."

"I know, Bob, I feel the same, but we've done all we can for one night. Go home and get some sleep. You've been on this since yesterday morning. Go home and get some rest.

Lemos hung up the phone and looked at his watch. He hadn't had any real sleep in over thirty-two hours. He walked over to the assistant fire chief, told him to thank the men and they would decide tomorrow what they would do next. Bob turned to Andy, who was still sitting by the coffee urn.

"We appreciate all your help, Andy, the coffee and rolls were great."

"Glad I could help, Bob. Sorry about the ruckus Duke caused." He pointed at the table saying, "Don't worry about the empty cups and all, I'll clean it up in the morning."

"In the morning? It's Saturday, the day before Christmas. You don't have to work today, do you?"

"Hah!" Andy exclaimed, shaking his head in discuss. "That woman that oversees the EPA around here don't care about that. Hell, since she's been around, they're on my ass all the time with that 'KEEP IT CLEAN' program she started. I'd better go check on things before I lock up. See you later." Andy was still rattling on as he turned out the back door.

Time: 1:45 AM

Bob drove home slowly. He couldn't get the search out of his mind. He wondered what he was missing. What was the clue? He unlocked the door to the apartment and looked at the clock over the television. It was 2:20 a.m. He flipped on the light in the kitchen, then looked down at the pictures lying on the table. *Sleep*, he thought, *I've got to get some sleep*. He picked up the picture of the Yates family thinking to himself, *You're a very lucky man, Mr. Yates. Beautiful wife, nice-looking son, the look of success.*

Lemos took the picture, opened the refrigerator and grabbed a cold Miller. As he popped the top on the can he rubbed it on his forehead, then returned to the living room. He didn't bother to turn on the lamp. He just flopped down in his easy chair. The light from the kitchen was still burning. Bob kept thinking as he looked at the picture of Yates holding his son on his knee, his wife hanging on to his arm, obviously taken at Christmas time. *You just can't disappear.* He yawned, took another gulp of Miller and yawned again. *What is the clue I'm looking for*...Yawning...Sleep.

Lemos awoke soaking wet with sweat, realizing he'd fallen asleep looking at the picture, hoping some clue would jump out from it. He looked around the easy chair. It had fallen on the floor beside him. When up picked it up, he smiled at Bill Yates with his son sitting on his leg. Then Bob saw it. The clue he'd been hoping for. Yates had his foot propped up on the step above where he stood, displaying a very expensive wingtip shoe.

Bob looked at the clock over the television. It was 10:30 a.m. *Holy shit, I fell asleep. DAMN! Where's that number to the impound lot?* He dialed in the numbers and waited for it to be answered. It rang five times. He hit the reset button. He grabbed the phone book from the coffee table thumbing to the S's, then the number. Bob hit the buttons and waited for someone to answer. "Come on, Andy, answer the damn phone!" It rang five times. He was about to hang it up when it clicked.

The voice on the other end sounded half asleep, "Hello."

"Andy, this is Bob Lemos. Last night out by the fence you said Duke found a shoe. Was the heel missing?"

"I don't rightly recall, Deputy. It was a nice one though."

"Was it a cordovan wingtip?"

Andy laughed; "Ah What? Hell, Bob, I ain't never heard of that company. Why do you ask?"

"Look, Andy, the evening after the Lopez accident I was out at your place. Duke had a shoe with the heel missing. You said he had a shoe also. What I want to know is, was it the same shoe or the other shoe of the pair."

"Got me by the ass, Deputy, I can go look."

"Never mind about that now. I need you to check that station wagon over good. I can be there in twenty minutes. Yates is still in that car."

As Bob was hanging up, he heard Andy calling, "Wait! Wait a minute, Deputy."

"Yeah, what is it?"

"It's gone!" The wagon went outta here two hours ago! You know, 'Ms. Treaster' the 'KEEP IT CLEAN' program. She wants all junked vehicles off the lot each week, unless they're being held for investigation."

"NO! Where'd they take it?"

"The closest scrape metal yard is out on Kings Highway in Kalamazoo. Hell, I hardly got time to scratch my ass since that bit..." Andy's statement died in the phone. Bob was on the way to the sheriff's office.

Time: 10:58 AM

Kin Kinnopplus was the duty dispatch when Lemos bolted through the door. "Kin! Get hold of the Kalamazoo police. Have them send a car to the scrape metal yard on Kings Highway. I don't know the name, but they will. Tell them to find a '51 Plymouth Station Wagon brought in this morning. Bill Yates is in that car!"

The dispatcher, without hesitation reached for phone saying; "I got it, Bob."

"I need a squad car. Are there any out back?"

"Take Murphy's, he won't need it. I'll patch Kalamazoo into our frequency. Take I-94, I'll have them intercept you at Portage Road."

Bob called out on his way to the squad car, "I can be there in twenty minutes!"

Lemos turned on the I-94 access ramp with the siren on and the lights flashing, thinking, *I hope we're not too late. I pray you're still alive Yates*, he told himself. He reached Westnedge

Avenue in twelve minutes and radioed his location. There were two Kalamazoo police cars waiting just west of Portage Road for intercept. They pulled out in front of him and he followed.

As they pulled into the salvage yard he aired a shy of relief. Waiting inside the gate was a Kalamazoo County sheriff's car, a Kalamazoo police car and an ambulance. Lemos was out of the squad car almost before it came to a stop and ran over to a uniformed officer standing beside his vehicle.

"Officer! I'm Bob Lemos, Van Buren Sheriff's Office. Have they found him yet?"

"No they..."

Bob looked around anxiously interrupting, "Where's the car?"

"No, we didn't get here in time."

Bob's heart hit the pit of his stomach like a ton of bricks. "What are you saying, he wasn't in the car?"

"No, I said we didn't get here in time to check the car before it went through the compactor. With it being a holiday, things weren't backed up so they took it directly from the flatbed. When we arrived the last one was going through the crusher. If we'd gotten the called just thirty minutes sooner, we might have..." Bob turned away and walked slowly to the squad car.

As he pulled out of the yard he couldn't stop a small tear from forming in the corner of his eye. He blamed himself for not seeing it sooner, for falling asleep on the couch. For failing a man he'd never met, but had become attached too. A kinship he had only felt with his Marine brothers. "I'm sorry, Colonel. So damn sorry."

Bob opened the door to his apartment and realized he didn't remember the drive back. He looked at the clock above the television. It was 12:30. The answering machine was flashing. Lemos pushed the play button. It was his ex. He was planning to be with his son and ex-wife at noon. They were having Christmas dinner together. Mary and Rick were going to her parents on Christmas Day. It didn't seem important anymore. He wasn't in the Christmas spirit, just exhausted. Opening the fridge, he pulled out the beer he'd started earlier, went into the bedroom undressed, finished off the beer and crawled into bed. He fell asleep telling himself to put it out of his mind. It was just part of the job, don't make it personal. But it was.

It was 1:25 PM when Bob heard the phone ringing. He picked it up. Before saying a word the sheriff was shouting, "HE'S ALIVE! Wake up, Bob, Yates is alive!"

He sprang to the side of the bed. What? Was he dreaming? The sheriff shouted again; "Bill Yates is alive."

Bob, awake now, couldn't believe what he was hearing, "How? Where, When?"

"About an hour ago. It was the dog, Sharpe's dog at the impound lot. It must have been last night sometime. I guess when the old guy, Andy, went in the shed to feed his dog, he found Yates on the dog's bed. He called 911. They said that Sharpe was there earlier this morning but didn't check on the dog then. It was late last night before he got out of the office due to the search and all. So he waited till noon to check the yard and feed his dog. Apparently, the dog pulled Yates out from underneath the car. They found a large hole where the wagon had been sitting. That EMS medic, Jessup, said if they hadn't gotten to Yates when they did, he wouldn't have made it. Anyway, I thought you'd want to know. Go back to sleep and have a Merry Christmas this evening with the family."

The deputy smiled, slowly hung up the phone and fell back to sleep.

Epilogue

A New Beginning

December 25th - Time: 10:30 PM

Bill opened his eye and tried to focus. He felt warm and he felt no pain. He could hear voices softly in the distance. The light was adjusting now. To the left toward the sounds was a doorway that light was coming through. He tried to move his arms, but they were strapped down. He looked up to see a plastic bag hanging to his left. He felt something touch his arm. Bill instantly recoiled, but then relaxed. It was a hand. A soft hand. One that he'd felt before. He looked up. It was Beth. She wiped his forehead with a soft cool cloth. Tears swelled from her eyes. Next to her was his son, Joe. As tall as his mother now. They were beautiful. For a split second he was afraid he would wake up and they would disappear. So many things needed to be said and so little time to say them. He knew his injuries were extensive, but he didn't care. Bill realized he'd been given a second chance. This time he wouldn't fail, them or himself.

His eye caught the glimpse of a figure sitting in the shadows across the room. It wasn't anyone he knew. Beth saw her husband looking in wonder and whispered, "He wants to speak to you, if it's all right."

Bill shook his head and in a raspy voice said, "Sure, is he the person that found me?"

Joe looked at the man motioning him to come up to the bedside.

"I just wanted to say, sir, you had no other option. I'm

Henry Jessup, the corpsman attached to your platoon with the 7th Marines in '91. You were a first lieutenant then. I'm sure you know what I'm talking about. That day has plagued my mind for years. I still see the anguish in your eyes when I told you I couldn't help. You had no other option." Then he reached down and touched the colonel's hand. "I know your duty was to your men and to not compromise the mission."

Bill replied, "Thank you, Jessup, but you're wrong. I did have another option and I took it. I failed and compromised the safety of my men and the mission."

"But, I was there, sir. I told you it was hopeless. I heard the shot."

Bill shook his head, "I couldn't do it. So I chose to do nothing. The boy pulled the trigger. He took control over fear with his final action. Even a decision not to decide is still a decision. There was another option."

Wm. C. Pond served in the USMC during the early years of the Vietnam Era. He retired in 2005 from his position as an operations auditor to live in Mount Pleasant, Michigan and a life of fishing and golfing in the summer, and reading and writing in the winter.

www.ingramcontent.com/pod-product-compliance
Lightning Source LLC
Chambersburg PA
CBHW020618130626
46552CB00003B/1024

* 9 7 8 0 6 1 5 1 8 1 8 3 7 *